W

never

slept

after

that

We Never Slept After That

A Novel

JULIANNA LEE

ISBN-13: 979-8-9918514-1-1

For all who shared their stories with me, and everyone who has a story to share.

Thank you for giving your words to the world.

Faleminderit nga thellësia e zemrës sime.

But First, Some Context:

On February 28th, 1998, the Serbians controlling the Federal Republic of Yugoslavia raided the villages of Likoshan and Qirez. Nestled in the center of Kosovo, a small autonomous province and now recognized as a country, these two villages were not alone. Serbian-led crackdowns on ethnic Albanian communities were not contained within the boundaries of a single municipality or a handful of homes. Muslim Kosovar Albanians, representing the province's majority ethnic group, faced targeted Serbian attacks in every corner of Kosovo.

If a single string tied together the lives of Serbs and Albanians, we would see this string stretch far, far, far back in time, their relationships interwoven in history from its very beginnings. Past the early 1990s, past the early 1900s, past the early 1300s even.

Take a glimpse back to the start of the decade, and we see Kosovo as the poorest entity of Yugoslavia, with the province's average resident making roughly $1,500 a year. The national average, meanwhile, was nearly four times that. Even before the war's onset, unemployment hit 70% of Kosovars, which only worsened after a post-war shift to a market economy despite the lack of foreign investment.

Formed to address discrimination against ethnic Kosovar Albanians, the Kosovo Liberation Army (KLA) banded together separatists whose begrudging toleration of Serbian control was nearing an end. Excluded from Balkan agreements ending war in the neighboring country of Bosnia, the KLA launched increasing retaliations only to meet the Serbian army's violent response. They were an army which made no distinction between grassroots rebels and everyday Kosovar civilians, a truth to which the destroyed homes of innocent Albanian families can attest.

Look farther back in time, and we come to the year 1389 and the Battle of Kosovo, pitting Serbian Orthodox Christians against an encroaching Ottoman Empire. The Serbs lost, with the Ottomans obtaining a Pyrrhic victory and both sides suffering from near-total casualties. When the Serbian commander Slobodan Milošević rose to power in Yugoslavia in the late 1980s, he capitalized on the battle's painful reminder to rally his people's nationalism and portray the vision of an ongoing struggle for Serbian survival.

From February of 1998 to June of 1999, Yugoslav Serbs displaced roughly 1.4 million Kosovar Albanians, laying waste to their homes and forcing many into lives dominated by the uncertain futures that loomed over their heads. In the span of these two years, 13,500 Kosovars died or went missing, with civilians representing three-quarters of the lives lost. The Serbians had sought to force out Albanians in the province, and they did just that.

Finally, after NATO interventions curbed Serbian military fronts in the summer of 1999, the Kumanovo Agreement formally ended the Kosovo War. The majority of Serbian forces withdrew from Kosovo, paving the way for reconstruction under the administration of the United Nations.

Born in Gjilan, Kosovo, Dimitri grew up as a young adult amidst a systematic campaign of terror against Albanians. Dimitri's voice represents dozens of Kosovar Albanians in their war torn home, their narratives compiled to form this single story.

And yet...

Any reader knows that no story is singular, and no story is stagnant. Hundreds, thousands, probably even millions of individuals possess the right to claim this story as their own. These individuals span countless countries, cultures, and centuries, yet cling to the same universal struggles and successes as the rest.

From the pages of one man's journey in one remote region of the globe, I ask you to allow this story into your mind, but not without your own revisions. Change it. Add your own narrative. Do not let it stand alone.

DIMITRI

***

There was very little in life that Dimitri questioned, and the fate of his village was no different. Like many other residents of Gjilan, he saw no way out, no possible chance of survival for the ones he cared about most. He had seen the Serbs in Bosnia, watching bloody scenes play out in newspaper headlines and hushed coffeehouse conversations. He was sure that Gjilan would be just the same… that *Kosovo* would be just the same, the invasion a cruel sequel of what had come before.

"Breakfast for Serbia." His father uttered these words with a twisted conviction. *That* was the fate of Kosovo, its people helpless at the hands of its neighbor. Perhaps they could not change the course of the war, the course of conquest. But they could face it head on, with a clarity so apparent that nobody could pretend they hadn't seen it coming. When the time came, they would not be shocked.

And the time did come. When Serbia hit, the whole village knew. One end of Gjilan to the other was probably a two-mile distance at most. The village center rested at the bottom of a hill such that, from all four corners of the village, you could see out to any part of the land. So, when Serbia hit, every mother and father and sister and brother peered out from their house to witness it for themselves.

It was all of a sudden, really. And it was everyone, even the children. The Serbs removed them all from the houses, assembling them into neat little lines and groups so uniform that they betrayed the sense of chaos that befell Gjilan. After they separated the men from the women and kids, they began to beat the men. Men who were Dimitri's age – twenty-three, maybe twenty-four–, and that realization was a scary one.

After that, some of the men took off into the forest and hid there for a day or two. Dimitri was one of them. They were escaping the Serbs, of course, but also escaping the uncertainty of what would happen next. In the woods, plans could be formulated, hidden speculations could spill out in the whispered sentences shared between men who could not protect their families at home.

In those early days, Dimitri's father was taken to the police station one day. Unlike the few who had fled into the woods, his father had stayed at home. If he had not, surely the Serbs would have noticed the absence of men at her house.

That day at the station, they had questioned him. "Your pistol?" They had asked, searching for the locations of things they could confiscate, power they could take from the people and keep for themselves. "Your shotgun?"

He returned home a while later to a house full of concerned family members and worried expressions. But he said little, and in doing so, there was much that he said. He never told his family that they had beaten him, and he never told them anything more than the obvious questions that they all had expected. Although Dimitri went to sleep that night with questions of his own, he never doubted for a second the motives behind her father's silence. Just as his father's report had been a tacit one, there was an unspoken understanding that his minimal words were a protection to them all, a blanket that shielded their inquiring eyes from the brutality of the interrogation.

They all struggled to sleep in the days that followed, their minds awhirl with anticipation and confusion and fear and regret. Days became weeks, and weeks became months, and still rest would evade Dimitri. ¨I'll never sleep after this,¨ he whispered to himself as his eyes slid shut one night, seeking sleep which would never come. In their respective bedrooms, his family members wished for the same respite, yet found the same sorrowful results.

They never slept after that.

***

Storm clouds supervised the town from above, sending down heavy streaks of rain to remind the people of its presence. The rhythmic pitter-patter on the window panes filled Dimitri's house with a gentle hum and replaced the family's otherwise-eerie silence. Nobody dared to venture outside that day, but not because of the weather. Truly, the torrential downpour knocking at the windows was a welcome substitute for the Serbs.

No, they were inside for a very different reason. Yesterday, a young boy went down to the village square. Perhaps he was escaping the stuffy atmosphere of a tense household, seeking solace in the center's fountain which spurted out water instead of shedding tears. Perhaps he was simply purchasing some groceries for his family, or a quick pastry to inhale on the walk back home.

Regardless, he never did make it back home that day. He never got to open his shopping bag, lining up toilet paper rolls and bags of flour on the table to pack away. He never got to wipe the trail of powdered sugar (dusting the hints of a growing mustache on his face) before he stepped inside to greet his mother and father and younger sisters. He never got to stare into the swirling water of the fountain, watching as the light drizzle of rain preceding tomorrow's predicted storm collided with the water's surface, *pluck-pluck, pluck-pluck.*

A Serbian officer shot him and he died.

Nobody knew how or why or when or who, but everyone heard the gunshot. Everyone saw the body lying against the fountain, a small pool of red mixing with the water in the basin.

Who knows what the boy thought of in these last moments? Did he feel regret that he had not picked another day to visit the square? Did he think of his family and his friends, or maybe a girl to whom his feelings would forever go unsaid? Would he face the afterlife with clenched fists, angry at a world which had brought him in just to take him out so soon?

What foreign aid Kosovo received, what equipment nations lent to this small country in need, the Serbs took. They came around to village houses, searching for what they could find so they could take it away. But potentially more destructive to the people, the Serbs took their hope. They sought out the peace shared by Kosovars determined to persist, and they squandered it.

No citizen of Gjilan had hope that day. They remained inside, nurturing that eerie silence. The silence that permeates places teeming with thoughts too inexpressible to be contained in mere words or sounds.

Throughout the history of Kosovo, this land had passed under the command of many rulers, trading hands so quickly that it could happen at any time if you didn't watch with a close eye. Illyrians, Thracians, Romans, Byzantines, Ottomans, Serbs, Italians, Yugoslavs, Serbs. They had all left their indelible mark on a people of ethnic Albanians residing in this stateless nation – now an autonomous province of Serbia, at least.

Dimitri knew that no nation could claim perfection in the unforgiving gaze of history. Each people – even his own – had fought and rebelled, persecuted and were persecuted. But especially in this region of the world, no two people clung to the same ethnicity, religion, social class, ideology, beliefs. Individuals and groups thrived and clashed, coexisted in a never-ending search for the points of harmony and disagreement amidst sharp divides. Now, although ethnic Muslim Albanians represented an overwhelming majority of all those living in Kosovo, the Orthodox Serbian minority dictated all government decisions, running the province with a strict grip over Albanian Kosovars.

Dimitri could recall one night seven or eight years ago as the family sat at the table for dinner. The memory lit up in his mind as he lay in bed, surrounded by the stifling sound of rainwater and narrowly-avoided silence. One seat had been empty at the table – his father's. He was late from work, to the surprise of a family that had never witnessed him this late for a meal together. The heaping plates of chicken on the table grew cold while the children grew restless and their mother grew worried.

His father had arrived a little while later, with a lost look in his eyes. He stood in the door frame for a minute, surveying his children and wife, who were just glad to see that he was safe and home. A brief pause, and then, with visible irritation, the words: "Why did you cook all of the chicken?" The family's confusion followed, conveyed in tilted heads.

"God, you weren't supposed to cook the entire chicken. Who's going to eat this? What were you thinking?" Their father thundered. It was the first and last time Dimitri would ever hear him raise his voice. As if embarrassed by his words, his father withdrew into another room, leaving them alone to eat. In the elapsed time, the chicken had become just as cold as his father's tone.

Well, maybe not *that* cold.

Later that night, Dimitri had pressed his ear to the thin wall dividing his bedroom from his parents' room, where muffled voices became audible with a bit of added concentration on Dimitri's part. "What are we going to do?" His mother's words. A pause, and then: "There are no jobs left… Not anywhere."

His father sighed, and Dimitri could imagine him rubbing his hands over the stubble on his chin as he always did when deep in thought. "I know, I know. You're right. I'll go into the city in the morning… see if someone there has any information or job they can offer. I'm sorry for this. I hope you know that."

"No," responded his mother. "Never apologize for what you cannot control. We will face it together, as we always have. But the kids cannot know. I don't want them to worry… They're too young." Just like that, Dimitri's father became one of the seven out of every ten Kosovars to lose their jobs amidst the economic downturn and unemployment following Serbian job dismissals.

Dimitri did not tell his younger siblings, and he assumed that his older brother Bledar would be informed in the morning. Bledar was always told these things. He was the smart one, the responsible one, the one anyone could turn to with a question.

The one thing Bledar could not do, however, was lie. Dimitri did not even need to ask Bledar if he knew. At the sight of the small bowls of soup for dinner the next day, the eldest child could not hide his pursed lips and darting glances toward his father. He could not help but cough, choking on his words, when he complimented his mother on an objectively tasteless meal. Of course, these subtle hints at abnormality passed over the heads of the younger children, but Dimitri noticed. He always did notice the little things, after all, even if his family didn't notice this unrecognized knack for detail that he possessed.

So Bledar *did* know. Dimitri had been correct after all. He never told Bledar that he knew. Instead, he watched for the small moments, the hushed conversations, the glances that would tell him all that he could possibly wonder. After a few months, his father managed to pick up a job in the next village over, one that did not even earn him a fraction of his previous salary, but that covered the basic costs. As conditions worsened over the years – as the shortage of goods became a regularity rather than an occasional nuisance – there became less of a need for additional cash to spend, anyway.

And now, here Dimitri was, lying in bed on the day after the young boy's death, thinking and staring at the ceiling as the storm outside let out no hint of retiring. Those days felt so far in the past that it was a wonder to Dimitri that he could remember them at all. Bledar was away fighting in the war now, and the family had no glimmer of an idea as to when he might return home.

Oh, how much he would have given to go back in time. Back to before it all, when he was a student, a soccer player, a person who could dream about anything and hear his mother tell him that he could achieve it.

He never had realized how much of a luxury it was, to dream.

***

Over a year passed. One day, Dimitri's brother Bledar came home from the war. After that, the family cried for weeks. Just one glance into his hollowed expression, one brush of hands as Bledar and Dimitri reached for the same cupboard handle, left pain igniting in the far reaches of his heart. Pain for the brother he once had, tears welling up into permanent pools in the corners of his eyes. It doesn't matter if they see you crying, in a situation like that.

They had forced him into the Serbian army for 15 months, forced him to fight for the same people who turned his home into a place of perpetual hurt. The war was in another city at that point. Knin, Bosnia. All of the Albanians served in the first line of duty so that, if one of them got the notion that he could fight fate and turned back, Serbs would have shot him. Shot him in the same head that harbored the ridiculous idea of escape. In Knin, Bledar fought the Croatians and Bosnians. But they had a signal, the Croatian army and the Albanians, so that they wouldn't shoot each other, wouldn't kill one of their own.

Dimitri wondered how many Serbs – how many innocent men possessing no hatred in their hearts for the Albanians they were fighting – were forced to fight like Bledar had been.

Serbs vs. Albanians. But it wasn't ever that simple, was it? Over the course of conflict, entire populations become reduced to two sides of a dispute, with a firm line drawn in the sand that can never be crossed. You are what you were born into, and that was that. You are at the mercy of your government, and you always were.

Much like when his father was taken in for questioning, Bledar couldn't say anything about his service. He couldn't tell them *anything*. Once again, the silence spoke wonders, pressing down upon the family's conscience like a weight that became easier to bear as time stretched on. It was hard for them all to see Bledar in this light, but Dimitri imagined it was heavens harder for their brother, who shouldered a heavier burden on his own. He had seen the world collapse just to have his voice taken from him.

That understanding was something Dimitri could not accept. That in the midst of it all, he should stay silent with the rest of them.

***

"I have to go," Dimitri told his parents one night, the four words accompanied by the screech of his coffee mug sliding across the counter as he pushed it away. He said nothing else. Nothing more needed to be said.

With pressed lips and a solemn understanding, his father nodded and coughed a little, trying to expel that notion that a father must always watch over his kids, always keep them within reach. His mother had seen it coming too, but she gasped nonetheless and allowed her hands to cover her face as she turned from her son. After a moment, she brushed her shaking hands across her cheeks and drew Dimitri into her chest for possibly the last time.

"You have to go," she murmured, assuring herself, assuring her husband, assuring Dimitri. "If you don't, they will come for you like they came for Bledar. And you might not come back." There it was, the real reason after all. Because it was a wonder the Serbs had not yet knocked on their door with Dimitri's name on their list, pulling him in to fight. His other brother and his two sisters were young, fresh into their teenage years. Not Dimitri.

At the end of the day, Dimitri had no choice but to leave. But it was better for them all if they pretended he had any say in the matter.

***

For 24 hours, Dimitri walked. Starting out in Gjilan, Dimitri left for a bus that would take him into the city of Presevo. To reach the station, he traversed rocky mountaintops where the only things that grew were wild grasses and dreams of escape. He was first in his village to walk these paths and brave these empty roads. Dimitri walked alone, as he knew he would, but he had not left without his father's promise that the family would leave at the first sign of *something wrong*.

An ironic word choice on their part, since everything was *wrong*. But that was their agreement: Dimitri would leave the next morning, and the family too would take off if ever they saw *something wrong*.

In Presevo, Dimitri had only one thing to look for: validation that the rumors were true. He heard that a group numbering close to a thousand people would set out from Presevo, but in those days, nobody could be sure of anything unless the anything was danger. He had heard that there would be a leader among them, to take them at midnight out of Kosovo to flee the war.

When he arrived at the bus to Presevo, he got to work hiding all that he brought with him. It didn't take long, because he only had two things with him. After constructing two doubled pockets within his jacket to conceal his passport, he slipped in the money he had: 50 German marks, the currency of choice over Serbian dinars. Once he twisted the pockets and adjusted his jacket to ensure that the coins rested silently when he walked, he boarded the bus. Each time the vehicle lurched over a rock out of place in the road or ground to a stop to take in more passengers, Dimitri's hand came to his side, as if to protect his meager belongings from revealing themselves.

At the border of Presevo, Serbian troops stopped the bus. They forced everyone outside and into rows, just as they had done in Gjilan on that first day. One by one, they took each Kosovar to the side, shouting, "Where are you going?" until they reached an answer that would satisfy their suspicions.

When it was his turn, Dimitri was careful to execute his rehearsed response in a genuine manner, slowing his words and stumbling over parts of his story just a little so as not to betray his true intentions. "I'm going to visit my family," he croaked to the Serbian guard, a short man with short balding hairs on his head and a piercing gaze. One of his fingers was wrapped in a slightly-bloodied bandage, but Dimitri trained his eyes on the man's face and did not look away.

"And where does your family live?" Eyebrows raised, the Serbian guard did not believe Dimitri, and they both knew it. Dimitri offered up the name of the main street in Presevo, one that everyone would know and one that Dimitri had traveled upon in happier days. He knew nobody who lived on that street, much less any family members, but he prayed that the guard would accept his excuse and move on to the next person.

The ends of the guard's mouth turned down as he slipped his pen and paper back into his pocket, nodding to himself as he moved on without another word. And just like that, Dimitri was free to board the bus again.

Setting out again an hour later, all of the men and women on the bus noticed that there were two seats newly empty. One seat was formerly filled by a young man like Dimitri. Nobody knew what happened to the two absent passengers, but nobody dared to ask or even enter the question into conversation with the people beside them, for fear that their inquiries would be punished in some way.

Occasional talking did fill the space in the vehicle, as time loosened the lips of nervous riders seeking solace in the shared anxieties of their neighbors. After tentative conversations, the three men seated behind him revealed that they were headed to the same meeting place in Presevo, the same rumored location that would bring a group of Kosovars into Macedonia.

It was fate that brought the four of them together, Dimitri decided, for one of them brought the others to an old man's house, an illicit resting stop for many of the travelers in Presevo. At midnight, the old man awoke those sleeping and bid them farewell as they set out to rejoin the throng of people embarking on foot to Macedonia.

So the rumors were true. Dimitri tossed this sentence around in his head for the early hours of walking. When he grew tired of this activity, he looked down at his feet, matching the strides of the hundreds around him. They all ascended the same hills, all pressing on in pursuit of the same mountain that would bring them ever closer to the neighboring country.

Shortly into their mountain climb, Dimitri startled at the sound of a soft crumple. A body's crumple as it collapsed to the ground, its existence confirmed by a sharp cry from the person to

Dimitri's right. In the dark, Dimitri fell to his knees, his arms reaching out, searching. His hand landed on the wrinkled skin of an overturned palm. *An old man, then.* As the crowd of people pushed on, ever forward, Dimitri used his dwindling strength to hoist the man up and against his shoulder. He waited there for a minute, allowing both of them a short break before continuing the trek. And in that minute, although he could not see it, Dimitri felt the old man's gratitude as his rapid inhales began to steady. A brief cough, an abrupt, "Thank you." And they moved on.

The night draped over them all, smothered them at times, vanishing the worry from their faces and concealing just how many were in this group. Without light and in the confines of the woods, they saw nothing. For ten hours, in the middle of the forest, they saw nothing. They wished they could look into each other's eyes and memorize the faces of their companions, but they saw nothing.

Until they saw the Serbian army. Then, they wished they could see nothing at all, nothing ever again.

The Serbs lay waiting, waiting, waiting just for them. It was silent then, too silent for the number of people in those woods. Each held his breath, as if the quiet would strike a bargain with the dark and collectively it would all make the Serbs forget they were even here.

As it turned out, a deal *had* been made after all. Not with the quiet and the dark, but with the army and the leader of the traveling group. The leader was a man named Bekim, whose raspy words disappeared into the wind when he talked, leaving his followers straining to pick up the missing pieces of his blunt sentences.

This time, though, there was no mistaking what Bekim said. The news etched itself forever into the minds of Dimitri and the others, forever into their horror-stained hearts, because each believed it to be the last news they would ever receive. Not just from Bekim, but from anyone at all.

"If you would like to pass this army and make it to Macedonia," Bekim grunted, "you must come forth with your money. If it is enough for the Serbs, you may go. If not…" He stopped, unwilling to waste his final sentence on a crowd who knew all too well what would happen *if not*.

A bribe. Heads bowed as if in defeat, men rushed forwards with the small sums hidden in their clothes, while some shrunk back in their pennilessness and prayed that they would remain out of notice. When it was his turn, Dimitri passed his 50 German marks into the hands of Bekim, who pocketed some for himself before returning the remaining coins to the bag he held aloft.

There were too many men, but not enough money. Time doubled and multiplied, folding in on itself and repeating until Dimitri could hardly take it anymore. Finally, the group dispensed their final coins, and the Serbs collected all that there was. They counted it, conferred with one another, and passed knowing chuckles that cut like daggers.

"It's not enough," a Serb called to Bekim. He was just loud enough that the front rows of Kosovars heard the words, and these men turned to those behind them and recounted the verdict. *It was not enough.* This message ruptured the eerie calm that previously overtook the group, inciting a fire of disbelief in its place.

For Dimitri, this felt like the end. He was never one to give up, never. But he was also never one to pretend. When, as kids, his friends in the village played imaginary games in the woods and shared laughs while constructing toy soldiers from twigs, Dimitri practiced. Since his first game with the older players in Gjilan, Dimitri nurtured one love: soccer. He filled dinner table discussions with each harrowing detail of the latest match, filling school lunch breaks with dribbling drills. In fourth grade, he became the captain of his team and the unofficial best player in the entire village. When there wasn't much to do in those days, there was always soccer. But even when there *was* something to do, if it wasn't soccer, Dimitri wasn't interested. Soccer was his one-way ticket to everything he wanted in this life, and that list never changed: fame, fun, friends, food for his family.

But as he grew up, he began to notice the cracks in the sport he loved. Without the coaching or the resources or the financial support to compete internationally, there wasn't much room to grow. When this new reality came crashing down, displacing the reality that Dimitri believed to be his soccer career, he never stepped foot on the fields again. And the next year brought whispers of war anyway, so that was that. There was *no* pretending in war.

To believe that this life would give him a second chance, a chance at all, was to pretend. Deep in his heart, Dimitri knew this, and so did the rest.

Then Dimitri felt a tap on his shoulder as a hoarse voice behind him asked, "What are they saying? My hearing, it's not what it used to be." It was the old man, the one who had fallen several paces back. Dimitri assumed they had been separated in the crowd over the many hours that followed, but the two had unknowingly walked the long journey together, side by side through it all. And now, as chaos took hold of them all, this old man was beside him again.

"The Serbs… they need more money for us to pass. But there's nothing." Dimitri felt his emotion well up, near overflowing in the comfort of this person he didn't even know at all. "We have nothing."

No response at first. Then, a gentle laugh. It became louder, a stark contrast to the loud conversations that came from the crowd, conversations riddled with dismay and concern. Dimitri listened, horrified, to this old man filling the space between them with a twisted happiness. He didn't know what to say, so instead, he allowed the laughter to continue. He believed he was doing the old man another service at this moment, giving him the time he needed to process what was sure to be a collective end for them all.

Instead, the old man reached into his jacket, withdrawing a bulging rectangle of rough leather that he pressed into Dimitri's hands. Turning it over, it felt like a wallet, but Dimitri would not accept such a hasty – or such a happy – conclusion. Frustrated with Dimitri's delay, the old man snatched it back and undid the clasp to reveal the stacks of German marks within. The two of them could just make out the numbers on the sides of the papers, and flipping through, Dimitri knew the sum to be at least 2000 marks, probably much more, definitely much more.

"How…" Dimitri's mind whirled with the possibilities. The possibility of what might have happened had the old man not gotten back up, not stayed with Dimitri on the arduous walk, not acquired such an incredible amount of money. The possibility of what the Serbs would say after this added bribe would make their army thousands of marks richer.

The old man interrupted it all, bringing Dimitri back to reality. "It doesn't *matter* how," he retorted with an almost imperceptible edge of bitterness, as if Dimitri's surprise was a slight. "Just go. Give it to them."

Dimitri nodded and pushed through the thick web of people, getting closer to Bekim and the Serbs with each step. "I have it!" He thrust the bills into the air, his very own white flag of surrender. "I have the money."

Years passed in the moments it took the Serbs to count the marks. Decades passed as they consulted one another, the meaning of their dialogue lost in its hushed nature. Millennia passed, and Dimitri held his breath for every second of it.

"Okay."

One Serb nodded, tucking the money into the satchel attached around his waist. "Okay. The money is good." He looked at Bekim, and Bekim looked back.

"They can all go."

***

For the next 24 hours, Dimitri continued on, but with a purpose. In the crowd, he lost sight of the old man, and this tormented him. Dimitri's *thank you* was left unsaid, and he carried this *thank you* with him as he scanned the outlines of faces and passed from one small group of people to the next. But the old man was nowhere to be found. All Dimitri could do was hope that the old man could muster the energy to push onward.

Making his rounds to a new group, Dimitri searched again for the old man. Instead, he found a woman with three kids. Walking alongside her teenage son, she balanced a toddler on her hip and dragged her other son by the hand. Not much older than seven, the younger boy struggled to match his mother's pace, who yanked his arm up occasionally, encouraging him to liven his steps. The mother's arms burned, and her eyelids drooped at times when she felt the burden of sleep press heavier on her limbs.

When she saw Dimitri, an unspoken agreement passed between them. Dimitri hoisted the younger boy onto his shoulders, and for ten miles of walking, the boy remained there, holding on as they traveled across stretches of mountains and rocky cliff edges, patches of grass and fields of sleeping peonies. In any other circumstance, these views may have been enjoyable, beautiful even.

At the border, the Macedonian army lay waiting. Another army intent on returning these men and women, girls and boys to war-town villages and disrupted homes. However, this was an expected army, patrolling the strip of land that marked the beginning of their country as every border police would do.

When the dots of Kosovars appeared on the horizon, the Macedonians sped off in their cars, racing toward the refugees as they scattered into ditches, woods, anything. Dimitri took off running. The boy on his shoulders held on, his feet *thud-thud-thudding* against Dimitri's sides. It was a soothing rhythm, a consistent *thud-thud-thud* that matched the frenzied pace of his sprinting. Sprinting into the adjacent woods, a sparse layout of trees that hardly provided hiding for the 15 or so people seeking solace in the forest.

As he crouched behind the base of the widest tree, the young boy's mother approached, hands outstretched to retrieve her son.

"Good luck." It was all Dimitri could say, all there really was to say at all.

With a brief nod of appreciation, the mother and her three children disappeared behind a collection of shrubs in the distance. Peeking out from behind the brush, the young boy raised his hand in Dimitri's direction, closed it into a fist, and opened it again. A small gesture, but it filled Dimitri's heart for a moment, and he sent a prayer up into the air: *Please, Allah, protect this boy. Keep him safe.*

After the Macedonians had passed, Dimitri resumed walking again, down to a strip of land in a small Macedonian village where trailers were gathered to bring the refugees into the larger towns. Dimitri's relative Qemal lived in Kumanovo, so he boarded the trailer leaving for the city.

After arriving in Kumanovo, Dimitri sunk into the embrace of his extended relatives, sunk into the embrace of their spare bed that night. His stomach was full, having eaten his first complete meal in two days.

Two days passed, and the time came to leave. Getting through each day was hard on them all, with war burning holes into family savings and making it that much more difficult to pay for necessities. Dimitri could not become a burden any longer, as much as his relatives begged him to stay for just a few more days. He could not put it off anymore. His undetermined future hung over him, and he could not bear living his life on hold as unknowns occupied every empty space in his mind.

That night, Dimitri entered into another round of goodbyes, setting off for the refugee camps not far from his relatives' house. Qemal had offered to drive him, a welcome rest for Dimitri's weary legs. They passed the time trading old memories and inquiring about extended family, but after a while, quiet overtook what had become forced conversation and Dimitri's eyes began to slide shut. Noticing this, Qemal encouraged him to rest, not even reaching the end of his sentence before Dimitri withdrew into a moment's sleep.

His slumber was short lived at best. An hour later, Qemal's vehicle ground to a halt, the car's hideous screech echoing throughout the night. Dimitri's hands flew to cover his face, to protect himself from whatever caused the abrupt change in motion.

"Sorry," Qemal muttered his apology as he threw the gear into park, his eyes trained on a figure walking in the opposite direction on the road. "We're fine. It's just…"

Dimitri blinked once, twice, and focused on the silhouette ahead of them. There was no mistaking it.

In unison, Dimitri and Qemal uttered one word: *"Ismail."* They threw open the car doors simultaneously, not bothering to shut them or survey their surroundings before getting out. *"Ismail!"* They shouted, racing toward the teenage boy in the black sweatshirt who had frozen in his tracks at the sight of the two men. Realizing that the boy must fear the two shadowy figures rushing towards him, Dimitri called out their names, "It's me, Dimitri! And Qemal."

Dissolving into relief, Ismail relaxed his tense shoulders and began to laugh. Dimitri and Qemal joined in as well, overcome with incredulity at the chance encounter. "My cousin," Dimitri called, wrapping his arms around his younger relative and pulling him in. Just that morning, Qemal's family had asked about Dimitri's first cousin Ismail, who Dimitri explained had come to Macedonia just two weeks before, to a different area well removed from the outskirts of Kumanovo. To see Ismail here, now, washed Dimitri with waves of confusion and gratitude. To see his cousin again felt like a gift, a sign that they were all on the right path, a better path.

"What are you… How…" Ismail, although no longer frightened, had more questions formulating in his brain than he had time to ask them. Instead, he waited for Dimitri and Qemal to resolve his uncertainty. Dimitri recounted his departure from Kosovo as quickly as possible, and peppered the boy with questions of his own when finished.

"Why are you in Kumanovo? We thought you had settled by now. And how is your sister? Have you seen her? Do you need food? Have you had water?" Dimitri forgot to breathe, talking until his cheeks reddened and Qemal swatted him on the back of the head.

“Enough already,” Qemal chuckled. “Just let the boy speak.”

And while Ismail provided context for his own late-night appearance in this street of Kumanovo, narrating the story of his delayed leave and his change of plans and his safe sister, Dimitri listened, but not fully. As long as Ismail’s responses verified that he was okay, Dimitri did not care about the rest. He was just lucky. They all were, really. Lucky to be alive, lucky to be with each other again.

Because Ismail agreed to stay with Dimitri in the town’s refugee camps, the two of them drove with Qemal to the police station. They acquired a paper there that would validate their stay with Qemal’s family and grant them entrance into the American-run facilities. Finally arriving at the camps, it was Qemal’s turn to say goodbye.

“Make sure you get to America. Both of you.” Dimitri and Ismail nodded with conviction, because both of them knew one thing:

they did not uproot their entire lives just to stay in these camps each day, wondering what could have been had they braved the greater unknown.

Qemal turned back before getting in the car. "And good luck." That was all he could say. All there really was to say at all.

They arranged to meet with their two cousins there with their wives and children, fifteen of them all in total. All fifteen of them had the same last name, so the camps did not separate them the way that they would normally.

Through it all – through the sparse meals, through the threadbare clothes, through the flimsy cots underneath which mice would scurry in the night – the fifteen remained together. There was a sort of twisted comfort in seeing the ones you loved most share in your pain, but as soon as one of them felt this comfort, it evaporated, turning to shame. Because it was terrible, really, for your cousin's faces to become windows into your own suffering, and for your nieces and nephews to ask their parents questions no child should ever have to ask.

"Uncle Dimitri, when are we going home?" One of the children tugged on his sleeve, turning her face up to her uncle as he swept her up into his arms.

"Do not worry," he reassured her, forcing a laugh that cut deep into his throat. "It will be soon."

While standing in line for the shower, Dimitri would spend the hour-long wait dreaming of America. When the icy spray would sputter on and off, leaving him to shiver in the cold and wait for the water's return, Dimitri would dream of a country with warm water and plentiful meals. He dreamt of a country whose people would take him in like their own, shower him with freedom and fulfilled promises. He would attend mosque there occasionally, find a job and settle down in a nice neighborhood. America was a place where you do it all – a place where you could start a family and live a contented life.

He knew it would not be easy, this new life. And he knew getting there would be even harder. But he imagined his future to be just like the hills and mountain sides he used to climb as a child in the sprawling landscape just south of his village. In the moment, it was grueling work, tiresome at best. But after reaching the peaks, after looking out to survey all that he had ever known and all that he had ever climbed, the past became an exhilarating adventure. An exertion justified by a beautiful view.

It felt like this life was on hold in the camps, a lingering pause on the remaining chapters of his time in the Balkans. If he had learned anything, it was that time was too precious to sit still and accept less. But in case he forgot this lesson, his cousin's passing would soon make it obvious enough.

***

Ismail fell sick in those days, taken to frequent bouts of coughing fits and fevers. *A violent sickness*, said one cousin. *Unfortunate symptoms for such a young boy*, said another. To the family, it was an issue of sympathy and mild concern. Although they certainly pitied his condition, nobody doubted for a minute that he would recover. *It's just a cough*, said one cousin. *It's just a fever*, said another. Ismail himself, although dismayed, possessed no great terrors about the matter, for was prone to similar ailments in years past and always fared just fine.

But this time was not like the others, and when Ismail lay down to sleep one night, he did not arise the next morning.

Silence befell them all as the sun peeked over the clouds and Ismail did not peek out from the covers. He remained there, the sun having fully risen to the tops of the sky. He remained there, the covers having been drawn back by a curious cousin who sought to wake Ismail up for lunch, since he had slept through breakfast. He remained there, as a family of fifteen became a family of fourteen, and as the fourteen gathered around his cot to clasp their hands in prayer and wail for the young boy.

"He went to his death, and nobody knew it," Dimitri released his pangs of regret with these words, allowing the shame to fill the empty spaces in his mind and heart, pricking him with cruel pains as he went to bed each night. At least, he *attempted* to go to bed. A more accurate description of Dimitri's nights would be one that recounted the tossing and turning, the headache that sent waves of nausea to his stomach when he glanced over at his cousin's empty cot for the third, fourth, fifth time.

It was when a newcomer occupied Ismail's bed that Dimitri did not feel himself any more, could not process being anywhere that was not home. And he knew, also, that home was the only place he could *not* go. He could not stay here anymore, though, and he began to notice that others felt this same agitation, this same distaste for the in-between state that was life in the camps.

"I've decided to leave next week," Dimitri announced to a group of men at the camp. Men who had become friends, friends bonded by circumstance and mutual respect for what it had taken just to get to this point. "I cannot stay here any longer, and I have to go back to say goodbye to my parents in Gjilan before I leave." The men nodded passively, their expressions taut and their faces filled with a somber understanding. It wasn't absentminded, this response of theirs. Rather, it was a trained response, the typical response when a man in the camp announces that he cannot stay in the in-between.

One man, however, perked up at the mention of Gjilan, his eyes alighting in a moment of recognition and rare hope. "And I am going to Shillovë tomorrow. My brother will be waiting for me at the border to bring us across into Kosovo. Prepare your things today, and we can leave together in the morning."

It was settled, then. Although one day wasn't nearly enough time to encode his cousin's faces into memories for eternity, to catalog every laugh and every tear he shared with each one of them in his mind before departing, Dimitri knew it was the only way. It didn't take long to pack his things, because there weren't any. So he spent those last hours with his family. It was the only day in the camps that seemed to pass quickly.

In the morning, Dimitri embraced his cousins, not knowing if he would ever see them again. He grasped the hands of his nieces and nephews and wished them well in their studies, instructing them to obey their parents and love their siblings and work hard for all of the things that they deserved but had yet to receive from a world that had turned its back on them. That last part he kept to himself, though.

"My biggest fear," he said to them, his voice barely above a whisper, "is that you will grow up believing that you do not belong, that God has not looked upon you with favor in this life. But do not feel inadequate because of the place you were born or the religion you practice, the language you speak or the struggles you have endured. If anything, it should be a source of pride to you. A source of strength, because you have been through it all, and you have come out on top. How many of your future classmates in America can say that, huh?" He turned away then, so that they could not glance at his face or catch sight of the drops that fell to the ground.

As he left them, he promised he would see them soon, and he wondered to himself whether this would turn out to be an expected lie or a miraculous truth.

It was the hardest thing he had ever done, to say goodbye.

He set out with the man going to Shillovë, and spent the long walk and drive wondering about his parents. Wondering how his parents would react when he told them that he was leaving for America. Wondering if his parents would have news to share with him. Wondering if his parents were even alive at all.

They passed the Macedonia-Kosovo border but didn't make it far before the sight of tanks and American troops dotted the horizon. Men in uniform occupied the streets of the city, and Dimitri craned his neck to understand what it was they were doing. Their car crawled forward, approaching the swarm of soldiers and civilians clogging the road in front of them. Finally, when it was clear that the car would not be able to get through, the car came to a stop.

Dimitri rolled down the window and motioned to an older man in plain clothing to get his attention. "Hey, hey!" he called, waving his arm until he received a worried glance directed his way in return. "All of this… what is it? What's wrong?"

The old man's brow wrinkled when he looked Dimitri up and down, as if he couldn't believe that anyone could ask such a ridiculous question. “You didn’t hear?” A laugh, cold and brief, punctuated the end of his retort. “The Serbs, they killed three Kosovars here. These troops are trying to clean up, I suppose, and we’re all just watching. What else is there to do these days except watch people clean up the messes they make?” Before Dimitri could respond, the old man turned away, disappearing into the throng of people.

It took some time, but finally the road was cleared, and the two could continue on to their homes and families.

They arrived at Gjilan first, as Shillovë was just another fifteen minutes northeast of Dimitri’s village. Dimitri could not thank him enough, this man who had brought him to the only place in the world that he wanted to go, even if for a day. “*Gjithë të mirat*.” He wished him well as he withdrew from the car, entering his home after what had seemed like a thousand eternities.

It was peculiar, how similar it looked. Here was the village fountain, its crumbling stone a place of respite for schoolchildren and a gathering place for gossiping mothers. Here was the bakery, where Dimitri would purchase late-night tullumba with his girlfriend, talking about soccer and school and the future between bites of fried dough. Until they broke up, that is. Even then, Dimitri would come some days to pick up tullumba to eat himself, sometimes taking it back to the soccer fields to share with his teammates. Here was that soccer field, actually. It was all here, except for the people. The people must have been inside, for there was nobody at the fountain, nobody at the bakery, nobody on the fields.

In the years to follow, his little village would become a city, with tall buildings breathing down each other's necks and popup businesses competing for store space downtown. But for now, Dimitri saw it as just the same as it had always been, and for that he was grateful. It was a dreary day after all, with the clouds assembling above his head and perhaps scaring away anyone from stepping foot outside today. That's what he told himself, that it was just the weather. The children would be out tomorrow. The mothers would be out tomorrow at the fountain, and soccer games would resume again. He wouldn't be there to see it. No, he would leave the next day. But it would happen, he was sure of it.

After he arrived at his house, he raised his fist to knock on the door, *one-two, one-two*. The seconds hung in the balance. He waited for his parents to open the door and stare for a minute, to welcome him in with shrieks of surprise and happiness, to fill his arms with hugs and plates of koftë. But he also teased the possibility that they would never come. Perhaps they died, or moved, or simply didn't feel like taking back someone who had left his parents once and was planning on leaving again.

Luckily, heavy footsteps approaching the door yanked these worries from his mind, filling him instead with a rush of eager anticipation. Dimitri's father peered out from behind the thick wooden frame of the doorway, a mess of dark hair covering the shock in his amber eyes. Before he could release his son's name from the tip of his tongue, the two fell into a hug, making up for the distance that kept them apart for far too long.

And then his mother was there, the three of them clinging to what they could have lost but didn't.

"Why are you–" His mother asked.

"How are you–" His father asked.

"What have you been–" Dimitri looked back at his parents, before allowing his question to die away just as the ones before had.

They disappeared into the sense of understanding that permeated their joyous reunion. In the end, there was no question that needed asking, because all was known already. His mother knew that she may never see her son again, or at least not for some time. His father knew that Dimitri had to leave, even if his parents could not. And Dimitri knew that they understood, that they would accept his departure with grace and a twinge of regret, regret at not being able to control the world.

The next morning, after the three exhausted their memory with endless retellings of childhood memories and exchanged endless mental souvenirs, they said their farewells. Before Dimitri left, his mother adopted a strange look in her eye. That look when you have something to say, a story to tell that has been told many times before but never loses its luster.

"When I first married your father –," she started, pausing to swat her husband as he groaned aloud at the beginning of the frequently-told tale, "I left everything I had known to move here. My family back in Albania didn't understand how I could leave their village – a home where nobody left, not ever – for a new life somewhere else, with someone else. How could they understand? We didn't have much, but we had each other. My parents never could grasp how that wasn't enough for me. They thought that I wasn't happy, that I wanted what they couldn't offer. Money, maybe a change of pace, or just a chance to get away.

"But what they never knew was something I never explained to them, really. I moved to Gjilan because I *was* happy back home. By the time I reached adulthood, I had lived a full life there. I experienced all the joy that could have been found in that small town because my parents gave it to me so freely. They kept no opportunity from me, and hid no wonders from my eyes. And that type of love made me content, but curious. Curious about what other joys I could find outside of my village, and what other wonders I could uncover all on my own. My childhood in Albania allowed me to realize how many things I could love about the world, so much so that I wanted to see more of it. And I wanted to see it with your father, someone who wanted that just as much as I did.

"Your situation is different, obviously. You're leaving Gjilan because you *can't* be happy here, and you need to go. It is what's right. But I beg of you, think of it also as a chance to experience a new happiness. A greater love. You will see so much in America that you do not understand, and you will miss the Gjilan that once was, but find what you can love about it all. I know you will, just… Don't forget that, okay?"

Her story had taken on new meaning for Dimitri. Had her words always sounded so sincere? Had her move from Albania to Kosovo always stirred such emotion deep in his heart? He longed to see things the way that she did. There was a delicacy to the way that she loved life, facing the world with a combination of tender concern and unabashed fascination. And now, riddled as she was with worry for her son, she showered him with sweet optimisms and unwavering reassurance.

Dimitri recognized all this and more. How could he begin to capture his gratitude? How could he convert years of security under his parents' care into neat little thank-yous echoed aloud in conversation? He left them that day with these two sentences:

"Thank you for giving me a home that is worth missing. Thank you for being a family I hate to leave behind."

As the sun rose in the sky, he too began a similar trek upwards, ascending the mountaintop that would lead him out of Gjilan. It was the second and last time Dimitri would ever leave. This time, it was for good.

Two days after Dimitri, it was his parents' turn. After watching their son disappear into the distance, they witnessed their will to stay in Gjilan vanish with him.

"Before it is too late," Dimitri's father whispered, his eyes still fixed on the diminishing figure, "we must also go. I once had the feeling that we couldn't possibly leave this place and start again, not at this point in our lives.

"But you're right." He turned to face his wife now, searching her face for a sign of approval before continuing. "You did it before.

Leave your home for something new, I mean. I'm willing to try it, if you are."

Dimitri's mother breathed out an exhale of relief as she leaned her shoulder against her husband and scanned the horizon. "Let's be gone by the end of the week. We've heard the rumors that there could be an attack in Gjilan soon. It's not safe here anymore, and we have a lot left of the world to see."

So they packed up their things and left.

When Dimitri's parents left, the scent of their freshly laundered clothes still lingered inside their now-abandoned house. Traces of flour from his mother's pita still clung to corners of kitchen cabinets. The bowl in which she crushed dried red peppers lay discarded on the counter.

Dimitri's parents departed Gjilan on a Thursday. Friday passed, and then came Saturday. And on that Saturday, Serbian troops attacked the village. The "rumors" were true, after all. Serbs came in swarms, hideous gnats that descended upon the village square and swept the grounds for hints of hiding Kosovars.

But by the time that they took Gjilan, there was nobody there to take. Word had reached all ears in the small village. One by one, each person had packed their things and moved on, knowing well that if they stayed, they would be dead by morning.

Perhaps the Serbs felt confusion in this terrible moment, that the only things left to destroy were houses never again to be inhabited. Homes that would never again welcome a soul inside its walls. No person would sleep in these beds. No person would sip coffee at the kitchen table while flipping aimlessly through an old newspaper. No person would hear the chidings of a mother reminding her child to leave the soccer ball outside where it belonged, to not bring that dirty thing into a house she had just cleaned.

Perhaps the Serbs, with their spare time, explored these houses, taking what they could find from refrigerators and jewelry boxes.

Inside Dimitri's house, even. Listen closely enough, and they might still have been able to hear the crackle of the sizzling *qebapa* on the grill, sear marks running along the sides of the sausage.

Dimitri did not know these things, nor would he ever know. If he had, would he have turned back? Would he have raced home to find his parents missing, knocking on that thick wooden door until his knuckles grew weary? Would his fruitless search have corrupted his mind with a neverending sense of restlessness, a dangerous thing for a young man soon to find himself in a new country?

But enough questions. Curiously-shaped question marks have dotted these pages too many times to count, and it takes no genius to understand the uncertainty that gripped Dimitri in those days.

Only time would predict the remaining scenes of Dimitri's journey. For now, he could only hope and pray. And dream.

***

"On behalf of the crew and our airlines, thank you for flying with us today."

The flight attendant flashed a brief smile as she concluded her welcoming words. Around Dimitri, passengers on the plane were buried in their books or newspapers, closing their eyes or staring idly out at the tarmac through the window. Nobody returned her smile, and nobody listened to her words with any particular amount of enthusiasm.

Except for Dimitri, of course. His eyes flitted from one thing to the next, alighting on the buttons overhead each seat and the workers dashing to and fro outside the plane. He peered (almost rudely, but this he did not know) at the men and women on board, wondering what reason could possibly bring every one of these individuals all of the way from Skopje to Boston. Macedonia to America.

It did not take long for Dimitri to understand that he was the only newcomer of them. These men and women, families and couples and individuals, had all flown before. Clearly. They would have been more interested if not. They would have been more like Dimitri was, fascinated and confused and worried all at once.

When the American soldiers running the Macedonian refugee camp booked his flight, he had expected to fly with at least one other migrant from his camp. Or at least from Kosovo at all! But no. It seemed as if Dimitri would be completing the final chapters of his journey alone, without the comfort of a companion who knew just what it had taken for him to be there. That was okay with him, though, as long as he could find his way to America and find his way to a place where he could settle down.

"We hope you enjoy your flight."

And they were off.

The plane raced down the tarmac, roaring in his ears. It was how he felt inside. A loud roaring in his heart, a feeling that thrummed and came alive all at once, a collection of every bit and piece of his life that collided to create this moment in time, just for him. He gripped the ends of his seat until his knuckles matched the shade of white coating the plane walls. Nothing about this felt natural. No, it was all forced into place.

And then they were in the sky and they were soaring, and everything Dimitri had ever known faded into ant-sized dots and then disappeared into nothingness, relegating his entire life to mere memories that time would twist and corrupt into half-truths and forgotten moments.

Despite a level of fatigue that pressed heavy upon his chest and jumbled his thoughts, Dimitri could not find the sleep that so evaded him. Instead, he filled his mind with pictures of the people he would meet in America and the places he would find greeting him at his arrival.

He imagined skyscrapers, black boxes stretching up into the clouds so that, even if you craned your neck just so, you still could not see the ends of them. He imagined people, adorned with leather boots and cowboy hats and plaid button-downs, chewing on lone pieces of straw as they laughed over jokes with strangers. He imagined city landscapes brimming with men and women always in a hurry, always going somewhere that was neither here nor there.

After the plane landed – a horrifying experience for Dimitri, who thought that the aircraft had just about broken with the noises it made upon contacting the ground – they did all of the normal things that were not normal to Dimitri in the slightest. They collected their luggage, of which Dimitri owned an embarrassingly minimal amount, and departed to their respective destinations.

Dimitri watched as a young man fell into the embrace of a girlfriend who sobbed at the sight of flowers in his outstretched hands. He directed his eyes to a mother greeting her children with arms open wide. He followed the noise of laughter to witness the exchange of two friends with sweatshirts sporting the same college name, two college roommates together again at last.

It would be a lie to say that these things did not hurt Dimitri, did not creep up on him and wash him with an unwanted feeling of loneliness in a place he could not call his own. But it would also be a lie to say that Dimitri did not expect it. It was a blessing, he knew, to be here at all and to have made it so far. But it did not make this feeling go away, nor did it make it any less valid.

Dimitri *was* met with a welcome of his own, however. A man with jet-black hair and a tightly-wound scarf stood off to the side in the airport baggage claim, hoisting up a printed piece of paper that read in bold: "WELCOME DIMITRI TO BOSTON."

It was the Albanian man working with the American charity, the agency extending immigration services and housing to the few lucky enough to receive it. Dimitri was one of the lucky ones, and for this he was eternally grateful. I mean, coming to the United States with nothing more than a few dollars to his name, how could he not be?

When Dimitri saw this sign, a smile broke across his face, the simple message absolving a small portion of that isolation he had been trying so hard to push aside. He waved in the direction of the man as he approached, who greeted him with a cordial *"Përshëndetje."* Dimitri returned the hello, diffusing as much gratitude as he could into his words and thanking the man for everything he had pledged to do.

“We are waiting to pick up another, but his flight doesn’t land until seven. He’s from Kamenica. Not far from Gjilan, eh? You two should have plenty to talk about.”

Dimitri brightened at these words, relieved to have someone he could face this newness with, who would understand it as he did. And as he waited with Petraq, the Albanian man whose somber tone and reserved personality melted away with hours of conversation, Dimitri began to feel as if he had *two* people with whom he could share these experiences.

As Petraq asked about Dimitri’s family back home, Dimitri peppered him with inquiries about American food and sports, cowboys and skyscrapers. “The language, too,” added Dimitri as he raised the pitch of his voice, mimicking the accent of the family next to him on the plane, “sounds like a car in traffic. It starts and stops, starts and stops, and there’s all this noise to it.”

“There are so many words here that I still cannot pronounce,” laughed Petraq as he looked out at the sea of flight-bound

Americans. "Like, *waterfall*. It just sounds so wrong." Dimitri practiced the word a few times, his mouth forming a hesitant O-shape and turning the syllables over, before he shook his head in amused confusion. "But you'll learn the language with time. I mean, you kind of have to, right?"

Before long, Petraq motioned to a man in the distance, a short man with thick eyebrows and eyes that crinkled at the corners when he smiled back at the two men. This was the other Kosovar, Arben. He was just as relieved as Dimitri had been to find company in this unfamiliar place, with its unfamiliar people and unfamiliar customs.

After Dimitri and Petraq introduced themselves to Arben, confirming that he had a safe flight and gathered all of his possessions, they were finally ready to see their new world for themselves. Walking over to the parked car, Petraq began to tell the two of his plans for their first days in Boston. "You both can stay in my guest bedroom for a couple of days while our agency finishes prepping your apartment. You'll be sharing it with two other Kosovars, but they won't be getting into Boston for a few days." With a click, Petraq unlocked the car, helping to hoist their suitcases into the trunk. "The apartment is just outside of Boston, in Lynn."

How surreal it all was to Dimitri, that he could nod at these words and accept them as truths, that he could begin to embrace a dream that was always just that: a dream. Of life in America, where he could sleep knowing that there was nobody waiting to drive him from his home. Of life in America, where he could afford to have all that he had lost, do all that he couldn't back home.

"No cowboys," noted Petraq as he motioned to the people outside of the airport, Americans wrapped up in black puffer jackets and sporting small glimpses of frowns on their faces.

"What could be so important," Arben wondered aloud, "to make them hurry the way that they do? People must always be late to their appointments here, I'd bet." Dimitri chuckled at how ridiculous they looked as they hurried every which way, mustering all of the concern in the world just in their concentrated expressions.

It was a strange place, this America, a land so full of contradictions. Everything stood out, so everything fit in. Gray washed over every inch of highway, draping itself over clouds and skyscrapers that obscured the rays of the sun above. And yet, splashes of violet and fiery orange and emerald green brought every bit of life to Lynn, adorning mural scenes on street corner shops and office buildings. Murals of shooting stars and young poolside crowds and men strumming guitars, a glimmer of hope in their eyes.

Meanwhile, men holding cups of steaming coffee stood next to men jangling cups full of coins on street corners, while women carrying briefcases passed women hoisting signs in the air, requesting donations. Strangers would avert your eyes or harbor poorly-concealed scowls on their hurried walks to something better, but their standoffishness was a front for the cheer that filled rooms at the donut shop next to Dimitri's apartment or the convenience store a few minutes downtown. People were stiff here, until they weren't. It is better, Dimitri decided, to seem cold and be warm, than seem warm and be cold.

"Certainly different," he had said on the phone one morning when Petraq called, inquiring about his first week in America. He remembered that first night, when Arben and Dimitri had spent the evening testing out kitchen appliances and television channels in their apartment, a dreary and cramped space they found to be spacious and inviting. How daunting it all seemed, to venture out into these streets. When other Kosovar migrants moved in over those next two days, each newcomer seemed to ease Dimitri's mind for a moment, for each person's presence pledged to Dimitri that he would not be alone in his confusion. There would always be someone else to feel the way he felt, to speak the phrases of his own language, and to venture out into these streets together.

“It is a confusing thing,” Petraq explained, “to understand these Americans at times. You will find that they are lost in their own dreams.” When Dimitri pushed his friend to tell him more about this strange concept (he had had no dreams to get lost in, after all), he was met only with: “I cannot explain it. I do not have the words. But after you have finished your language lessons and can understand English properly, get to know one of them, any of them. You will find that they simply cannot give up their dreams, even for the length of a coffee chat or an afternoon stroll. Those dreams will always be there with them, even if you don’t expect it at first.”

It would take the passing of many months for Dimitri to catch a glimpse of understanding in this matter. When this day would come and this would happen, he would not be able to unsee the truth in a people very much lost in their dreams, desires, wonders, would-be’s and could-be’s. He would come to see them sagging under the weight of lofty ambitions that had gone unfulfilled for so long, people’s hearts pulsing with the dizzying and exhilarating combination of dissatisfaction and hope.

Perhaps this explained why these men and women always had somewhere to be, always had a justification for their hustle and bustle and the gates that closed off their hearts to unfamiliar crowds, leaving only reservations for the onlookers.

But get to know one of them, any of them, and Dimitri would find that familiarity was the key to unlock those gates, revealing a life brimming with dreams of all kinds. Like the single mother of two who lived next door, dreaming of the day she could pay the landlord on time, dreaming of the day she could send her children off to school without concern that they would leave her behind like her husband had. Or like the elderly man who ran the pizza place down the street, secretly hoping with each ring of the restaurant's phone that it would be his daughter calling, at long last breaking thirty years of radio silence.

While obviously there were exceptions, as there always are to any rules, Dimitri never heard of these rifts between families before coming to America. Perhaps differing dreams drove these Americans apart, and having dreams was the prerequisite to personal conflict that explained its absence in Kosovo. In Kosovo, everyone wanted similar things, and they wanted them together, not alone. If a family member in Kosovo didn't have a place to stay in the days before the war, you would take them in, not allowing them to spend the night sleeping on a bench outside.

He hadn't expected this perfect country to have financial struggles, either. He was surprised to hear that many couldn't afford what he imagined to be easily obtained in America: a home, an education, a doctor for your kids. After he had realized all of this – which, again, took very many months – he would think back to his earlier days and question what made them all believe that America was a perfect place.

In many ways, though, it was. Worlds better than his last months in Kosovo, although that was a dangerously low bar. The best way Dimitri could explain it was that there were things to be taken for granted here. That was a phrase he learned quickly in conversation: *"taken for granted."* When he asked the middle-aged woman who gave them English lessons what it meant one day, she struggled to frame it in a way that he could understand. But later, Dimitri would come to learn that it was a sort of assumed privilege, a failed recognition of everything in life that was going well. Food, work, health, safety. Going to bed at night with the utmost confidence that you would wake up in the morning, free from the looming threat of an inevitable invasion weaseling its way into your dreams and subconscious fears. Nobody took these things for granted in Kosovo. Many times, they didn't have them at all.

After a month in America, Petraq found jobs for Dimitri and the others. Dimitri's work paid a meager $5.50 an hour, but at least it was something. Everyone in the apartment was given a $50 stipend, and then Petraq broke the news. The agency could not finance their expenses any longer, and they would need to afford rent with the money they made at their jobs. What extra cash they had seemed to vanish within seconds after grocery shopping runs and laundromat costs, so Dimitri couldn't fathom holding onto the dollar bills long enough to pay a monthly apartment fee and keep the always-irritated landlord at bay.

He didn't know how it was possible, but he knew that they had to try. There wasn't any other option, really. His confusion paralyzed him at times, stopping him in his tracks when he reached out to take a bowl from the woman at the soup kitchen or hand over his last dollars to receive the plastic grocery bags of bread and deli meat. Deep down, though, he understood that standing stagnant for too long was a perilous decision in a country full of people moving quickly at all times. The rushing rapids would sweep him away and carry him along with them, going *down down down*, if he did not fight back and push on in the opposite direction of the current.

Never for one day would Dimitri forget that they had made it through onto the other side. He would remind himself of this just as he reminded the others each day, although none of them needed it. They all knew how lucky they were to be here and to be in this position, because they could not shake the glaring examples of the unlucky ones from their minds, examples that clung to the deepest depths of their being and begged them to live on their behalf.

***

On the day that they were to have their medical checkups, Petraq stopped by the apartment to drop off a map and show them how to get to the local hospital. “You take the train here,” he pointed to a red circle hastily drawn onto the flimsy paper, “and follow the road here.”

And then Petraq was off to a meeting of sorts, occupied by a world that demanded so much of him. That left Dimitri and the other Kosovars in his apartment, still a little lost and more than a little frightful of the underground train that everyone called, “the T.”

Dimitri had never seen one of these underground trains before, and he would soon realize that it's not good to start off with the T. Well, he did use a bus in Boston once, but it was different, and it was only one bus. Ever since Dimitri got to America, he became the unofficial leader of the newly-forged family of Kosovars all living in their apartment. Maybe it was because he landed on the first flight, or maybe it was because he was the closest to Petraq. Regardless of the reason, Dimitri would always be the one to collect their funds, remind Arben that it was his turn to get the groceries, and navigate their daily English lessons with the most determination (and success). That day, he would be the one to wield their map, and he would be the one to lead them to the hospital for their checkup. It was a thing they were supposed to do as refugees, Petraq had told them, "to ensure that you're healthy."

Dimitri and the others got off the train at one too many wrong stops, distracted by the overflow of passengers on board and the lurching movements of the train car. Although arriving an hour late to their appointment, they finally made it, and for this small victory Dimitri felt a rush of pride upon entering the hospital.

Although a weight upon his shoulders that intimidated him at first, serving as the group's unspoken leader for the past month was a refreshing change of pace. Since the start of the war, Dimitri had been living his life by responding to the actions of others, constantly under the control of Serbian invasion threats, field officers at the refugee camps, and his own fears. Now, he was still lost, but at least he held the reins. At least he had a hand in dictating his own story.

So Dimitri went into the hospital that day with his head raised, allowing himself just this temporary respite from his doubts, basking in the role he played in getting them there. Not just in getting them to the hospital, but in getting them *everywhere* they needed to go.

Unfortunately, his success would prove rather limited that day. After entering from the opposite end of the building and pursuing some questionable turns around cold hospital corners, Dimitri reached a corridor branching off into private rooms. He had yet to find the waiting room that Petraq described to them back at the apartment, and he was smart enough to know that they must have gotten lost along the way. Arben cleared his throat, clearly uncomfortable in a place where they could tell they did not belong. "Why don't you all wait here," suggested Dimitri, "while I try to find someone who can help us?"

How he would secure the aid he sought, however, was beyond Dimitri. Despite the vast improvements he was making in their English lessons, he could barely string together a sentence, let alone arrange the right peculiar words into the questions he needed to ask at this moment. He wandered further down the hall a bit, turning the corner just to find another stretch of doors along the walls, most of which were open to reveal the patients within. Dimitri looked in to find rooms strewn with empty wheelchairs and cast-aside television remotes, with the sounds of beeping monitors and laughing and crying escaping behind the few doors that were closed. Each room was another world, another life, and Dimitri was curious about them all.

Then he heard something that stopped him, gluing his worn sneakers to the vinyl flooring and preventing him from moving an inch. There was a woman in the room to the left of him, hurling French words at what Dimitri could only guess was an unwelcome audience. It wasn't the exasperation presenting itself so vividly in the delivery of her sentences that snatched up his attention, but the mere fact that he could understand what these sentences said. When he was born, Dimitri's mother fed him French phrases like they were a child's favorite snack, speaking the language so often that he had no choice but to adopt it himself. His mother's father had been a professor in France long ago, and he passed on to his daughter what he believed to be the most beautiful language of them all – and he knew quite a few. In return, Dimitri's mother taught him, and he always considered it a pointless thing to be able to speak words which nobody could understand. It wasn't much fun to have a talent that he could not share, young Dimitri had noted to his mother once.

But perhaps he *should* have thanked his mother, for surely this woman in the hospital would direct Dimitri toward his group's appointment if he asked her in French. He only hoped that it was not too late, that he might hear his mother's gentle voice over the phone one day and thank her himself for teaching him all those years ago.

Late though they were, Dimitri decided to wait a second, overcome with split-second indecision and the unavoidable interest he took in their argument behind the cracked door. In the room across from the French woman, an elderly lady threaded beads onto a string, stacks of the finished product piling up on her bedside table. Dimitri could not see, nor did his gaze hover for long, but I will tell you: she was adding the last beads to her tenth bracelet. One for each of her children, none of whom had come to visit her during her prolonged stay at the hospital. One for each of the ten daggers that had been driven through her heart when they did not show up in those months. And now, she was close enough to death that she could feel it in her bones and know that that day was her last. Her hands shook as she tied the knot on the tenth string, and when this was complete she knew that her life was as well. Bringing the beads to her mouth, she kissed them quickly, and her lips moved to say a silent prayer. She was ready to go, but not before she raised her eyes to make contact with Dimitri's upon hearing his movement in the halls, winking briefly before letting them close for the final time.

Dimitri smiled at the sight of this old lady, whose innocent craft had put her to sleep. While she napped, the French woman opposite her continued to wail in her room, until her pleading was curbed by a booming voice. "Josephine, please. You've had 52 chemotherapies. 50 blood transfusions. 7 surgeries. You're on your fourth line of chemotherapy!"

No response. Radioactive silence punctuated the air around them as the woman pursed her lips and pressed her fingers against the outline of bones along her temples. A sigh, and the man's words continued. "Look, the ethics team just wants the best for you. *I* just want the best for you. Your doctor has said that they can't do anything more to help you, and he's right. Why don't you want to spend your last days in hospice, with the family?"

At the innocent question, the woman lifted her head, an anxious fire relit within her soul. "Because I'm 42, that's why. I'm 42 and I have ovarian cancer and I did *not* spend four years in and out of this hospital just to be told I have six weeks left to live. No, I'm not giving up now. I'm telling them I want to live, but they're telling me they won't save me when my heart stops. That doesn't even make sense."

At this, the man's mouth formed a small circle, left open in shock. A second or two passed, and then he mustered the strength to return his own remarks, remarks he knew would crush her. "Your cancer has multiplied and spread all throughout your body. You're short of breath and suffering every single day, and if they resuscitate you under a full code order, you'll be even worse. It won't be a life worth living."

The man had no more patience left to give her. And so he left the room, failing to notice the conspicuous man in the hallway who stood facing their door. But Dimitri noticed him, in his loose scarf and patterned sweater, face reddened from what could have been shouting or emotion (or both).

Dimitri hung outside the room for a brief passing of time, looking back at the elderly woman opposite Josephine. Her eyes remained closed, a peaceful hint of a smile stretching the wrinkles that adorned her face. Surely it would be rude to walk into the other room now, after Josephine and that man had fought the way that they did. But time was a precious thing – Dimitri knew that better than anyone – and he didn't want the others to fear that he got lost or left them behind.

Knock-knock. A pause. *Knock-knock.* A pause, again. At last, a raspy inquiry: "Well, are you coming in or not?"

Dimitri swung upon the door. Josephine lay concealed under layers and layers of blankets, one hand draped over the pillows on her bed while the other brushed aside a stray curl that had fallen over her eyes. "I saw you in the hallway," she remarked, searching his face for a sign of what he could possibly have to say to her. "Who are you?"

Now it was Dimitri's turn for his face to redden, flushed in embarrassment at his poor timing. "Ma'am, please forgive me," he began, the French words starting and stopping and ending abruptly in their peculiar sounds. But it surprised Josphine nonetheless, who drew her head back a bit and nodded upon understanding that she would not need to attempt English for the sake of this unknown man. "I apologize for coming in at an unfortunate time, but I have a question. I recently came here from Kosovo with some others, and now we are trying to find the location of our checkup here. But we got lost, and none of us can speak English, and I don't know how to work this map, and I heard you speaking French and I just knew I had to ask you about…, or else we could've been…, and–"

Seeing the words fail him, Josephine cut him off, her original coldness dissolving into a welcoming grin. “Your French! It’s impeccable, really. And say no more, I understand you completely. Here, hand me your map and I will show you where to go. You’re in the in-patient part of the hospital now, but it’s not far from where you need to be.” She angled the papers towards Dimitri so he could see as she swept her hand in an arcing motion, connecting their current location to where the check-up would be held. After leaving a few instructions of her own, Josephine watched Dimitri relax upon knowing that he could once again lead the group.

Dimitri cupped his hands together and bent his head, showering down *thank you*s for her generosity. But as he turned to leave, he was met with the words:

“Wait.”

Josephine took a clip from her hair and deftly pinned a flyaway curl to the side of her head before she continued. “I trust that you heard me, right? Earlier, in the hallway. You heard our conversation?" Dimitri nodded, overtaken by a sheepish mien. "No, no, that's quite all right. We weren't particularly quiet, anyway. I was asking because I wanted to say something to you about it.

"I came to this country when I was a girl, probably around your age. I hadn't wanted to; my parents made me. I know your circumstances are much different, but I suspect you're feeling the same way as I did. Confused, certainly. Eager, perhaps.

"Do not forget this change for what it is: an opportunity. For you to take control of your life and tell everyone else to mind their business. There were many people who tried to tell me what I should be in this country – how I should dress, who I should marry, how I should take advantage of being in a place where dreams can become realities just as realities can fall back into nightmares. Up until that point, I had always been controlled. My parents, school, the normal teenage woes. So I didn't listen to any of them, and I was better for it.

"But now, in these last moments, I am once again robbed of having any say over my own life. Do not ever let that happen to you – and you must promise me that – because it will leave you at a loss when you die, grasping for the things you did for the world just to realize you did it all because you had to.

"And now, as I die, I cannot save myself. Even if it *is* the wrong decision, I should have been allowed to make it. I should have been allowed to make a decision.

"I need to know that you will make yours."

***

Months passed. Biting winter winds that tear at your coat and send numbness to your mittened fingers retreat into spring, where chill breezes ruffle pink peonies in city gardens and carry along blue jays in the air above.

When Dimitri was preparing to flee Kosovo – a time that felt like yesterday and a million years ago all wrapped up into one – he had been accepted to come to either America or Australia. He had chosen the United States right away. It was closer, for one. One of his relatives lived in Australia, an old man who turned eighty years old back when Dimitri was still a child. Before the war, he used to tell them stories about that country, bad experiences that Dimitri and his siblings didn't particularly understand and didn't particularly like.

So America it was, the land of dreams that revealed themselves on television screens and radio broadcasts, that permeated Dimitri's original expectations for an easy life here. The family never had any relatives in America at the time, so nobody could fact-check this assumption.

It was a good thing that he picked America. Three months later, Australia began to send the Kosovar refugees back. Six months later, they sent more and more Kosovars, back to a wartorn home, tantalized by a taste of freedom just to be delivered back into the hands from which they had escaped.

The best life ever. That's what Dimitri had thought it was going to be, and it would be, eventually, but it would take him almost 30 years. For others in his apartment, it would take far longer, and perhaps they would never even get there.

Now, though, a few months into his American life, Dimitri felt himself adjusting. He could read and write English very well; hearing and speaking was a different beast, one that would take him a little bit longer to tame. The Kosovars in his apartment became a family, still struggling to pay those bills but doing it regardless. The constant work became dependable, so at least there was that. And there was no shortage of wonders in this city, so Dimitri never ended his days with that dull feeling of wanting more that creeps into every young adult's mind at some point in their lives.

Dimitri had called his family for the first time, too. He couldn't quite recall the specifics of how it all happened, because, frankly, he didn't care. He only cared that it happened, that he called his uncle in Switzerland one day over the phone and heard his parents say his name another time, his mother hollering joyously and his father laughing to push away the tears.

Dimitri was using one of those phone cards at the convenience store, the ones you have to scratch. $5, $20, like scratch tickets.

The card allotted him only 15 minutes to call outside the country, so Dimitri channeled months of emotion into his sentences, ensuring the health of each of his family members back home before providing his worry-stricken parents with a report that pleased them. It killed him that he could not reach across the phone and draw them into his arms, proving to them that *he had made it.* It killed his mother that she could not see him for herself, assess the state of the dark circles under his eyes and feign admonishment over an overdue haircut. It killed his father that he could not clap his hands on his son's back, beaming with pride that Dimitri did what they all could not do.

But it was just a phone call. Just a phone call, and yet they poured everything into those 15 minutes, knowing they might not get this chance again for a long while. Dimitri eagerly informed his parents of the checks that he would be sending them, his plans to one day buy up some land in Kosovo and build them a new house. He didn't know it yet, but he would do all this and more, fulfilling every promise he made to them.

***

It was really spring now, this late May day at the beach. The waves churned and clashed and tossed themselves upon the shore, receding back just to rush forward again with renewed vigor. That was the captivating part, Dimitri realized. They always came back, battering each grain of sand and rock lining the infinite stretches of coast with the same determination as before. Yes, Dimitri knew that was the nature of the thing, but he couldn't help but envy the consistency of the rush. It was dependable. It never failed.

Dimitri reached down to pick up a sleek black rock, running his thumb over the object’s surprisingly smooth surface, its former roughness worn down by years and years worth of waves. How many turns about the earth had this one small stone taken? How many tides had claimed the object as their own before they lost interest, returning it back to life on land?

Dimitri stared out at the blue-green sea until a voice drew him back to reality.

"Are you going to skip it?" A young woman around Dimitri's age called from behind him. She had been walking along the water's edge, but stopped when she saw him examining the rock. When greeted with his silence, she motioned toward his hand, undisturbed by the lack of response. "The rock. Are you going to skip it?"

Dimitri shrugged his shoulders and turned up his palms, confused. "My English is… bad." He smiled an apology, allowing his thick accent to speak for itself.

The young woman – her name was Emma, though Dimitri didn't know that yet – nodded in understanding. She opened her mouth as if to say something but closed it, offering up the most imperceptible shake of her head. She looked as if she had something to say, but could not say it. Dimitri watched as she took the rock from his hands and proceeded to chuck it into the ocean. Mild anger quickly replaced his bewilderment as he watched the small streak of black soar, cutting through the wind on its way toward landing in the water. *Perhaps it was another odd American custom*, he thought, *to take what is not yours from the hands of others.*

But instead of disappearing under the surface of the waves with a dissatisfying *plop*, the rock skimmed along the top, jumped across the waters, and danced over frothy white sea swells. Dimitri faced Emma with eyebrows raised. He wanted to ask her how she manipulated the stone into performing this trick, into challenging the waves and all their dominance – but alas, he did not have the words. He couldn't have asked, anyway. Just as quickly as she had appeared, she was gone again, sprinting to catch up to her friends as they resumed their walk on the beach.

Dimitri came back the next day. Same time, same spot. He was determined to figure it out on his own. After nearly half an hour, however, Dimitri had coated his fingers in sand and coated the ocean floor in pebbles, representing every failed attempt he made to skip a rock. When he couldn't find another stone to throw, he turned around, accepting defeat and beginning the walk home.

He turned around, stepped forward, and collided with the young woman from yesterday. "Më fal," Dimitri gasped, for he did not know how to apologize except in his own language.

Emma held her hand to her head, but her grin remained. "S'ka problem."

She knew it yesterday, recognizing it in the melodic staccato of his syllables and over-enunciated vowels, and so she had come back the next day to teach him how to skip rocks properly… in Albanian.

Dimitri froze upon hearing the words roll off her tongue so easily. “You’re Albanian?” He whispered, as if fearful to wake himself up from what seemed so much like a dream. To have a person understand both the world he came from and the world he was entering was more than he had ever expected from someone here. Yet Emma was this person.

It might not surprise you to hear that, after a handful of very short years together, Emma and Dimitri married. But I’ll leave it to you to imagine their personal anecdotes and private conversations leading up to marriage. Surely you didn’t think this was a romance book?

Some days, Dimitri would think back to when he had picked up that small black rock on the beach. Just as the waves would always pull the rock back to sea, Dimitri felt then that Kosovo would always pull on him, begging him back to the only home he had ever known. Now though, he knew this to be untrue. There was no one path for him – no, there had *never* been one path for him. It was wrong for Dimitri to have assumed that he was a stationary rock, constantly thwarted by the plans of selfish waves who grabbed and never gave back, or at least never returned what they took back to their origins. In this new land, he learned to take control, find himself, find others. In this new land, he learned to skip along the surface of the waves, performing a dance that resisted the ocean's clutches, if only for a little while.

***

Grocery store cashier. Packaging company employee.

Hairdresser. Model.

It's not the path most people take toward becoming a doctor, but it was Dimitri's. He started off by ringing up customers at the local grocery store, taking home paychecks that seemed to get spent before he pulled out the keys to his apartment and stepped inside after a long day at work. It was an honest job, and Dimitri did it well – so well, in fact, that it was impossible for his manager not to notice who he could be.

Calling up a chain company in the area, his manager secured for him a full-time job in delivery and packaging. Which meant… a car. A brand-new, company car. Not the best, but it was to Dimitri, especially when he learned that, for his 17 years of work, he wouldn't spend a penny of his (now increased) pay on gasoline. That was gold, and his apartment family rejoiced at Dimitri's new role as their part-time chauffeur, bringing them to appointments and interviews and events without so much as a hint of a complaint.

Thanks to Emma, Dimitri learned English well. She would quiz him on the words he learned from his morning language lessons and pour over the mail he received, reading aloud advertisements for upcoming events at the local cultural center and discounts at the convenience store and acting classes at the modeling school downtown. Their routine continued until Dimitri could read the mail himself, skillfully navigating through dependent clauses and marketing abbreviations until Emma chuckled and shook her head in disbelief at the remarkable progress.

One day, as he picked up the latest pamphlet from the modeling school – how the school could afford to send such frequent mail,

Dimitri would never understand – and hovered his hand over the recycling to discard the spam, he froze. He couldn't bring himself to watch the red and white letters disappear into the bin's sea of cardboard boxes and torn envelopes. Instead, he read over the words again, and wondered whether it had been a sign all along. Work at the packaging company was going well (and paying well), but his job hours were shorter than at the grocery store, leaving leftover time to make some additional money to send back home.

So he did it. He went to modeling school, and after that he went to hairdresser school, and after that he cut hair and went to modeling shoots on the side for five or six years, anything to survive. He took every opportunity, really, for he never turned down the chance to earn extra cash for his family. Finally, he was taking control, making the decisions that he had always yearned to make for himself. Just as the French lady from the hospital, Josephine, had encouraged him, although he needed no encouragement in the matter. He never forgot her words, and he wondered whether she was still alive today. Deep down, Dimitri knew that she wasn't, but it was fine for him to wonder about these things because there really was no way of knowing for sure.

A social security number, green card, passport, citizenship, and several years later, Dimitri began to doubt the sustainability of it all. How much longer could he dash from one job to the next, when he was so ready to move onto a house, a family, a future life? He had the money, after all, but he lacked the stability that Emma sought from him before she would agree to get married.

"I've made every decision, but I can't seem to make this one," he admitted to Arben one day over lunch. "I don't know what I want to do next, even when every fiber of my being tells me that I am not content with where I am now. It's this in-between state I'm caught in, and I can't get out and move on until I figure out who I want to be." He had told all of this to Emma, of course, and they had puzzled through it many nights together, but no idea grew out of their conversations or flourished under their dutiful examinations of the many possibilities awaiting him.

Arben nodded, careful about what he could say next. "I might have an idea, but it would take a lot. Of time, money, everything. You'd have to give up so much." He drew out the length of each word as he considered how to frame his proposition. "You are always helping," he began, "driving us where we need to be or sending paychecks back to your family or watching over the finances when months are especially tough. And decisions… I mean, you said it yourself. You've gone to school for modeling and hairdressing, and you're a fast learner."

Dimitri raised his eyebrows, urging Arben to hurry to his point. "Okay, okay. I think you should become a doctor. You're always hung up over that Josephine story from the hospital all those many years ago. Don't you think that *means* something? Why her, of every person you have encountered and every story you've been met with? There's something special about it to you."

It was true. Dimitri still remembered the 50 blood transfusions that failed her, the four lines of chemotherapy that couldn't save her life. And he always considered it cruel that she should die at 42, that lives could be taken too soon. Her life or the thousands of Kosovar lives, the ones wounded in combat and the innocent civilians killed on the basis of their geography, ethnicity, religion. So many of them, had they received proper treatment and the medical care they deserved, would be alive today, maybe even here in Boston with him.

Dimitri tallied the numbers in his head. It would be a decade to finish everything, he reasoned. Undergraduate school, medical school, typically residency programs and fellowships too. But…

"I'll do it." Dimitri nodded, the corners of his mouth turning up and his eyes alighting with the realization that he had figured it out, that it was within reach despite seeming so far out of his grasp. "I'm going to do it."

And he did.

Of course he did! I told you earlier that his career path wasn't typical for a doctor. Maybe I shouldn't have spoiled the surprise, and for that, I do apologize. But I suspect you'll forgive me, because you probably never doubted him, did you? If I hadn't said he would succeed from the start, you would've believed it regardless, I think. Either way, he *did* become a doctor, and he did all the rest of it too: marriage, house, family, the whole nine yards. I'm going to flash forward a bit now, since I don't know what it really takes to become a doctor, though I know all I need to: it was hardly without its difficulties, but Dimitri did it anyway. The rest, I'll leave to you to infer.

***

"Doctor, may I speak to you for a minute?"

The oncologist from Floor 7 peeked her head around Dimitri's door, an urgent look replacing her typically unconcerned demeanor.

"Of course," said Dimitri as he rose from his desk, joining her where she stood.

"Sorry to be brief here. I've got a patient for you, name's John. Middle-aged man, Stage Four lung cancer. We've already taken care of him, given him chemo, surgery, all of it. Unfortunately, every treatment has failed, and his cancer has only grown through the rounds. He decided to be a Comfort Measures Only patient, so we're transferring him to you to live out his last month." Dimitri was nodding along with each one of the oncologist's words, jotting down notes onto his pad of paper as she recited the patient's facts. He was a palliative care doctor, so these types of cases were ordinary for him, although sad, of course.

"Oh, one more thing. And this is important." The oncologist glanced quickly behind her to ensure that the door was shut, blocking them off from any accidental listeners in the hallway. "There's a different last name for him in the system because of some security issues, but we're going to rely on using his medical number for confidentiality. I don't know the details and John won't share them with us, but it seems like he was involved in some court case a while back and has a restraining order out against an individual in the area. Like I said, I don't know for certain, but I do know that his privacy is of the utmost importance to our team.

"Anyway, I have to go, but thank you for all of this. John should be in shortly. Let me know if you need anything, although I'm sure you'll be just fine."

Dimitri got to work. Most times, two patients would be assigned to a singular room, but this time Dimitri set aside a private room for the new patient so that his family could be assured discrete visits if needed. He felt a rush of intrigue, having never before cared for a patient with a confidential name or case. Throughout the entire month of his attendance, he would never once ask John what had happened, what court case or restraining order or individual had prompted such clandestine care.

It's not like he was allowed to, anyway. The question would occupy his thoughts from time to time, but it wouldn't take long before Dimitri would forget it, his curiosity lost in the perpetual overflow of medical responsibilities and agenda items boring permanent tacks onto the bulletin board taking up room in that brain of his.

Finally, a knock came at the door. "Come in!" called Dimitri, rotating in his swivel chair to greet John and the nurse wheeling him in.

"It's nice to meet you." Understanding that his patient would be too weak to return a handshake, Dimitri rested the palm of his head on John's forehead, the typical greeting he gave to the ones that were as sick as he. They exchanged pleasantries – as much as John could afford to extend, that is – while the nurse propped him up into bed. With each movement, Dimitri watched as grimaces revealed John's fight to keep the pain at bay, this fight of pushing and shoving his sharp aches down until his facial expressions were the only things to betray his fabricated sense of calm.

Achieving rest in his stationary position in bed, John relaxed, which Dimitri took as his cue to begin the formal introductions. "I'm your palliative care doctor," Dimitri explained, "which means that I'll be focusing on your symptoms and comfort care. I see you've already had a lot of aggressive treatment and now wish to focus on the quality of your life. If you need something or are ever suffering, I want you to let me know as soon as you can, please. Think of it like a fire: if you can address the pain when it's at a more minimal stage, it will be easier to put out.

"I've also set up a private room for you, so you can have visitors and family members come at any time."

"That shouldn't be a problem," murmured John, rubbing his index finger over his knuckles repeatedly as he whispered the words. "I won't be expecting any visitors, anyway."

Dimitri nodded, unwilling to say anything that could jeopardize their relationship before it even began. "Well, I'm going to get you hooked up to a pain pump. I'm sure the oncologist has discussed this with you, but your lung cancer has spread to the bones. There will be a small amount of medication circulating into your bloodstream through your IV, and that will be continual. Again, it's small, and it's just to keep the discomfort to a minimum. But there's also a part of the pump that functions as a demand button, which you can press if you're in need of a higher demand dose. *You're* in control," – *unlike Josephine,* he thought – "and that decision is yours alone to make. You'll notice, though, that additional medication will cause additional sedation, so you won't be as lucid as you might be used to."

"Thank you," John responded, incredulous at the amount of warmth radiating from the doctor's kind words. He turned his palms up in a gesture of gratitude as he added, "And I won't be needing that demand button. If you could take it away so that I don't have the temptation, that would be wonderful." Dimitri, impressed by the patient's fortitude, agreed to do just as John asked.

Every time the nurse would come to move him in that month, John would clench his teeth, his jaw rigid in resistance against the pain. Occasionally, he would let out a sharp gasp or cry as she turned him onto his side, his heart rate quickening with the agony. Yet he never went back on his decision to live with the torment, choosing distress over the loss of his clear mind.

Over the next few weeks, Dimitri got to know John for the person that he was beyond the patient, beyond the cancer and the hospital bed and the medical check-ins and the pain assessments. John felt like an old friend at times, asking about Dimitri's wife and kids when he stopped in to say hello each morning and tease John for neglecting to eat his breakfast (once again). Dimitri understood this man to be a proper comedian, always with a joke to offer up in their momentary lulls in conversation. Resilient, too, his strength shining through not just in physical displays but through the stories of his childhood in Albania.

Oh, did I forget to tell you? I'm sorry about that. Perhaps I may not be the best narrator, but at least I am trying my best at the matter. Yes, it's true. By sheer chance – although I don't believe anything in life is really the result of pure coincidence – John was Albanian.

He had made the sign of the cross one day, and Dimitri worked up the confidence to ask if he was Christian. One year into his job, and he still felt nervous asking his patients personal questions, for fear that he might use an English word incorrectly and receive a horrified look in response to his accidental offense. But his longing to uncover the story within each of them – *who* they were, what their heart beated for, what they dreamed up to that point in their lives – always trumped his lack of confidence, as it had this time.

"Yes, I am," John had said, pulling out the cross necklace tucked into his shirt. "Eastern Orthodox, though, not Catholic." He always expected the follow-up question and grew tired of correcting people, so he started providing his denomination before others got the chance to ask. He enjoyed watching the surprise and intrigue – sometimes disappointment – flit across faces when he would tell them this, but never did he see someone as interested as Dimitri to hear it.

"Orthodox? Are you from Europe, then?"

"Albania," John nodded. "The southeastern part, close to Greece."

"But your name…" Dimitri figured he must have changed it like many of the Kosovar migrants he had known, who rearranged letters into presentable packages for American audiences when choosing new legal names. They had been eager to shed the identity markers flagging them as outsiders to Americans who might turn up their noses at the peculiar consonant pairs and the two dots above the *e* and the *y* sounds that hid behind the sloping *j* at the end of a name.

"John doesn't give me away, huh? I changed the spelling when I came back to America in the '90s. It's supposed to be G-j-o-n. Same pronunciation, of course, but one look at the *g* and the *j* and everyone just gives up." Dimitri nodded sympathetically, but held his tongue.

"I was born in Boston, actually, but my parents moved us back to Albania when I was just two years old. There was something political about the reason they moved, something they had to handle in the capital, Tirana. Before I was born, my father had been some sort of politician or dissenter or something, an anticommunist one, but I never cared much for what he did. I never asked my parents what they thought about communism or Albania or America or any of it."

"Did you ever regret it?" Dimitri was hesitant to reveal that he, too, was Albanian. He wanted to avoid the inevitable conversation that would ensue, when John would ask where he was from and Dimitri would say Kosovo, and John would ask if he was Muslim, and he would say yes. He wasn't ashamed of his religion, not by any means. But he had only known it as a negative, especially to the Eastern Orthodox Christians he knew back home.

It was a complicated matter, religion in Albania. The country had been Christian until it was taken over by the Ottomans, who forced conversions upon a population that welcomed Islam over the untimely consequences of refusing. The southern section remained Christian for the most part, because of its proximity to Greece, so it made sense that John was from the south. Then Albania became communist and religion was banned entirely, although many practiced in hidden cellars and offered up secret prayers in hushed voices when nobody was looking. That was all over in the 1990s, a few years before the Kosovo War began, and Albania dissolved into political mayhem and corruption. To be any type of politician at this time was a peculiar thing indeed.

It was too bad, really, that Dimitri did not say that he was Muslim. If only he had, he might have found that John would receive the news warmly, asking questions about his family back home and commending Dimitri for surviving the arduous journey that was life in Kosovo. But you cannot blame him, of course, for staying silent. When you have spent your whole life exposed to one perspective on somebody or something, it is all you can be expected to know.

"Yes," John affirmed. "I always regretted not learning more about what my parents thought about the world. I knew about their lives, how they met, what months at sea on the voyage to America would have been like for my pregnant mother. It was an arranged marriage, but it must have been arranged well, because they never fought once in their entire lives. Not once did either of them raise their voice at the other, never. I wish I could say I'm as easy-tempered as they were. I knew them as people, but I never knew their minds. Especially now, with no family members that wish to call me their own, I wish I had taken the time to get to know the family I once had in my parents."

Dimitri looked away when he said this, and he asked himself not to cry, *not to cry*, *please don't cry*, pleading with himself to conceal his emotion for this man. But it was too late, for John, observant as he was, understood his doctor's look immediately. "You must understand," he prompted, awaiting an explanation.

"Yes and no." Dimitri coughed, warding off the tears successfully. "My wife is estranged from her uncle, and I know that that's difficult for her. But I – I have not seen my parents since I was a boy. Young adult, you could say, but I was a boy.

Not by my choice, and certainly not by theirs, either, but I know what it's like to take for granted a parent's presence. I have seen relatives and friends pass, and I have always regretted not hearing everything they had to say before they went, not asking every question I could. I have heard infinite stories from my patients as well, and they all say the same thing.

"Excuse me if I'm overstepping, but you've said before that you know you won't be here long. You've even said you don't *want* to be here long, that it will be your time soon enough. What's stopping you from calling the family that you have while you still can?"

John contemplated the question, emotion showing plainly on his worn face. "You're right about it being my time. I've said it before, and I feel it's even truer now. I'm tired. In pain. And I'm ready to go. But I just don't think I have it in me to call them. I've let too much time pass, and I wouldn't have the faintest idea of what to say or how to say it. And what would they say to me, after all these years?"

In this moment, Dimitri felt all the fire within him. He never understood any one thing to be as important to say as what he could say now. "You'll never know if you don't try. Obviously you can't control what they say. Control what *you* say. If I had the chance to say more before a loved one passed, I wouldn't give that up for the world.

"John, it's been said a million times before because it's so true: the best time is now."

They said their farewells, both of them knowing that these would be the last words ever exchanged between them. Dimitri arranged for John to see someone from the chaplain office so that he could receive a prayer for the dying, nondenominational unlike the typical Anointing of the Sick for Catholics. Speaking to the nurse in the hall, he pressed a hefty phone book into her hands, instructing her to help the patient locate his family members' numbers within the pages. Then he collected some things in his office, cleaning up the space for a while before leaving for the day.

On his way out, he was stopped by that same nurse, her breathing uneven from what seemed like her hurry to find him on his way out. "Doctor, one more thing." She placed a worn journal into his arms, a thick book filled with hundreds of pages, yellowed from the passing of many years. "John asked me to give this to you."

Dimitri thanked her and waited until he got in the car to flip open its cracked leather cover. A pink slip of paper from the medical pad in John's room fell out onto his lap. He rested the journal in the passenger seat as he picked up the note to read it.

"Nga një shqiptar në tjetrin, faleminderit. Lamtumirë."
[*From one Albanian to the other, thank you. Farewell.*]

Dimitri's voice caught in his throat and stayed there. The tears rolled down his cheeks, heavy now, years worth of grief and regret and longing and confusion marching in straight lines along his face. *How did he know?* He could not bear to read this journal now, this raw collection of John's life, so neatly bound within the pages of a book untouched and unread by the world. He started the car, eager to share it all with his wife, eager to read this with her at his side.

The sun had sunk beneath the earth when Dimitri's car pulled into the driveway, having endured a long stretch of traffic in an unusually poor commute home. An hour and a half of silence is what Dimitri allowed himself during the drive, and now he was ready to recount the day's events.

But he entered the house and found his wife crying, sobbing, sunk to her knees on the kitchen's cold and unfeeling tile floor. The children slept in the next room over, innocent, just as unaware of what tore at their mother as Dimitri was. He rushed to her side, holding her until she could look at him.

"My uncle," she murmured. "He called. And he's gone." It was all she could say. All that needed to be said.

As they embraced on the kitchen floor, it all made sense to Dimitri. Emma loved to talk, but her family was one topic she refused to discuss. Her mother died at childbirth, her father left, and her uncle raised her. He was all she had growing up. But they were estranged and had been for her entire life after childhood. John – this patient to whom Dimitri had become inexplicably linked for the past month – was that uncle.

Dimitri knew his wife. He knew that she had yearned for a call from her uncle for decades. And he also knew that she couldn't talk about that call with him, not yet. She needed to process it on her own first, and he could only be there with her, for her, while she did. There *was* one other thing he could do, though.

"Emma," he said, drawing back to pick something up off the floor. "I can explain all of it, but I know now is not that time. Your uncle kept a journal, his whole life. I don't know what happened between you two, and like I said, I'll explain later. For now, I hope this is enough." Eyes wide, his wife received the book into her arms, flipping open to a random page.

In all of those years, she had done so much for others. Take Dimitri for a prime example: she practically taught him English, encouraged him to become a doctor, watched over the kids and picked up extra hours at work so that he could do this one thing, so that he could create a dream and fulfill it. Now, he could do this one thing for her, this one magical thing.

"Thank you." She would not question how he came into possession of this journal. No, not now. For now, this was enough. For now, it was all she could say. All that needed to be said.

GJON

////////

24 June 1967

Name Day. Today I walked outside to expressions of pity from neighbors and lifted eyebrows from the elderly woman across the street. When I stopped into the bakery to pick up some bread for my parents, the baker gave me the freshest loaf and for free, but he had to ruin it all with that crinkle in his forehead and that look in his eyes. I know what he was saying, and he knew that I knew. If there were no consequences, he would have said *Sorry, Gjon, that you can't celebrate Name Day this year. Or any year after, for that matter.*

I still have birthdays, but those don't matter here. Your day is your Name Day, the day when mom makes dozens of dishes with those apricots, the ones with the little dash of liquor in them, and people come from all parts of town to hug you and kiss you and honor you. All day, the doors of our house would remain open, and all day, the people would come.

Today would have been my thirteenth Name Day. But we cannot celebrate it, because your Name Day commemorates the saint that shares your name, and we can't commemorate saints anymore. So I didn't wake to the ringing of church bells this morning. No carved wooden crosses from my cousins or the sound of my aunt and uncle arguing in the backyard over whether there were enough olives in the bread they brought.

It's been a few months now since Enver Hoxha and the communists have banned religion entirely. Nobody was shocked when Hoxha stepped onto that podium in Tirana and proclaimed that Albania would be the *first atheist state in the world*. Nobody was shocked because each year they had watched us more closely. There were more Albanians each year who joined the Communist Party, and fewer grumbling voices at coffeehouses complaining about the rigid rules and food shortages. Each Name Day, there were fewer neighbors who stopped by, fewer people who raised their heads in passing and greeted me with a smile and kind words on their lips.

There *was* one thing I received today: A journal. My father took me aside before bed and presented me with a book of empty pages (the ones I'm writing in now), telling me that he had snuck scraps of paper over the past year into his work satchel, saving them up just for me. He used to write Byzantine music and do political work back when I was very young, but now he works for a little printing company, making books.

I used to love his music, begging my mother to let me skip school for the day and listen to him work, hear his undulating tone bring life to the hymns as he hummed their rich and haunting melodies. I would adorn myself in my finest clothes for Sunday masses, enthralled by the ethereal chants that reverberated in the domed cathedral of our church. I felt we were linked in this way: My father, the church's president and the town's musician, and I, his son, the one who wanted to follow him and do as he did. I wanted to become a singer myself, feeling the familiar drone of each sustained note stir within me as my eyes traced the iconography of the church, the solemn figures who always looked back.

But things changed. Our church was converted into a museum, for one. A hilariously ironic thing for them to do, because a museum is supposed to preserve a culture and educate on it, not replace a culture with something else entirely. My father lost his job, of course, and instead of writing hymns, he worked to make books out of what others wrote, and there was no fun in that. The sun dips below the mountains, casting long shadows through our windows, and only then will my father return from his long days at work, having earned barely enough for us to make it through to the next day.

I'm not supposed to know any of this, any of the hardship, but of course I do anyway. I am the eldest, and so I make it my mission to know these things.

Anyway, as things changed, my dream changed. I figured that if I couldn't write songs to sing them, I could at least write something. I started reading the extra books my father brought home, pouring over the vivid imagery of faraway lands and elaborate plots – albeit heavily censored storylines. I see these books as windows into new experiences and mirrors reflecting my own curiosities, stories upon stories of things I can never see for myself, stories that will have to suffice in book form alone.

My parents noticed this and they became excited, thinking that an interest in reading and writing would encourage me to pay more attention in class. They were wrong, of course. I am smart most days, but I have no interest in the multiplication tables my teacher feeds us in the morning or the inclination for discipline that a communist education demands of us. There is no alternative to obedience, so I do as I am told, but not willingly, and I certainly don't enjoy it.

But back to this journal, this diary that is now mine and only mine, a future home to all that I have wondered and seen. At a time when everything worth knowing or keeping must remain a secret, I am glad to have this to myself. My *own* secret.

I will write in this book every day. Each morning – no, each night – I will sit down in bed and allow my words to flow across these pages, muddying them with the ink of my mind. It's getting late now, and I have work to do in the morning, so I'm going to sleep. But I will be back tomorrow.

////////

7 October 1968

My father died today.

I don't want to write about him. I don't want to write at all. In truth, I want to pick this book up and hurl it across the room with every ounce of rage that punctures my ribs and swells my soul. I can't bear to watch my words mix with tears on the page, the droplets accumulating until it looks as if I spilled my water across the lines. I hate to see the letters smudge in the way that they are now.

I didn't want to write, but I am anyway, because I have written in this book every night since my Name Day and I don't plan to stop now. I can't think about anything but him, although I don't want to talk about his death in any particular regard. So I'll tell you about him, my father.

His parents wanted him to become a doctor, but he would always say that he didn't have the heart. He couldn't tell them that he just didn't see himself taking care of other people's problems every day. Maybe that made him a little selfish – rather, I think that most definitely made him a little selfish. Anyway, he never had to make that decision, because his father died when he was very young (a cruel parallel, now that I reflect on it) and World War II started and the beginnings of communism crept into conversation, and you know the rest.

He grew up near here, in a small town in the south of Albania where men would sit by the sea and drink their coffee as women toted water in pails back home and did the laundry by hand. He also went to high school, which was pretty significant for his time. I think what was most notable about him, though, was how much he loved my mother. It's a dull thing to say, and I cringe a little as I write this, but it really is true, and if there's one thing I want to be within these pages, it is honest. My parents married in the June days following Lent, because in the Orthodox custom, you couldn't marry during that season of sadness and devotion and penance.

My mother is a little bit younger than my father, with a head full of chestnut-colored curls and a short stature that betrays her domineering presence. She has exquisite taste, and if anyone these days could afford to, she would purchase the most beautiful silk and linen dresses for my younger sisters. She would prepare meals atop tables set with the finest silver, china, crystal. Of course, none of that is possible, but you can see it all reflected in her standards, the high standards she sets upon herself and everyone she deems worthy of her love (which is a lot of people). My mother is an immaculate person who keeps an immaculate house. For every visitor that enters, she will take out a glass from the cupboard to prepare them some water. But first, she will wash the cup thoroughly for her guest, taking time to dry the glass so that it gleams from a fresh clean.

My mother's father had remarried a woman who was your classic stepmother archetype: traditional, mean, made her stepdaughter do all of the housework and cleaning and raising the younger children. She spent all the money that her husband made, and there was a lot of it, as my mother's father ran a lucrative business trading textiles and fabrics. My mother was ready to leave, and so she embraced the marriage her parents had arranged without a single question about her future partner. It would have been frowned upon, anyway, to question your parents' decision. Especially as a girl.

It is an interesting concept to me, this idea of tying yourself permanently to a person you have never met. All my father saw of my mother was a photo before he agreed to marry her. And in the times of my grandparents, you didn't even see the wife before you married. Some parents would plan future weddings before the brides- and grooms-to-be were even born.

The story of my grandparents and their wedding is what has really made me question the practice. I'm talking about my mother's father – the rich one, who worked in the textile trade – and his first wife, who passed away before he remarried my mother's stepmother. My grandmother's family presented the youngest of their three daughters to the parents of my grandfather. She was a young woman considered to be the most beautiful in the entire town, and the next town over too. At once, the wedding between their children was set.

In those days, the bride would approach the altar with a veil obscuring her facial features, so that the church could not catch a glimpse of her until after the couple had been married. Well, when my grandfather and grandmother were pronounced husband and wife, my grandmother raised her covering to reveal that she was not the youngest daughter after all. She was the eldest daughter, the less desirable one, the one her parents had tried to marry off for quite some time but to no avail. It wasn't uncommon for parents to deceive in this way, but my mother always made it seem as if this put a strain on their relationship before it even began.

My parents are good people. Really, that is all I can say. All I know about them is their backgrounds, if I'm being quite honest, but that is all I need to know to say that they are good. Charming, hospitable, generous, honorable. Humble, smart. Nothing fake about them, no pretenses to their kind smiles and hearty laughs.

But I can no longer pretend that my unimpressive sentences are taking my mind off of the pain that gnaws at my heart now, or the shaking that has snuck into my fingers as I clutch my pen. After each paragraph, I've paused to rub my index finger over my knuckles, back and forth, back and forth, as I always do when my anxiety seems to overtake me. So I might attempt a new strategy now and seek sleep, although I don't know how rest is possible now. How can my bones rest, when my mind whirs with the power of a thousand winds?

////////

3 November 1968

Today is the first day that I struggled to remember what it was like for my family to own a telephone. I had gone down to the village square to make a call, but I stopped walking for a minute when I realized that I forgot what it felt like to hold a telephone in my hands and call it my own. (Or rather, my family's.) I had to close my eyes to see its smooth black surface, light that streamed through the windowpanes glinting off its shiny exterior. I heard the steps of passersby skirting around my frozen figure as I attempted to recall hearing the ring of the telephone from my bedroom upstairs. I would always race to be the first of my siblings to pick it up and press my ear to the receiver, but I don't race anywhere anymore.

A lot of things are forbidden these days, telephones being just one of them. You can't get meat, or if you can, it's not more than a few ounces every month. You can't drive a car, and you certainly can't travel from town to town without a passport and a very valid reason for your entry into the next village over. You can't receive mail without the Party receiving it first, crossing out conversations unfit for Albanian eyes and ears. I know that last part because we got our Christmas letter yesterday, the one our distant cousins in America send each year. This time, just like the past two Christmases, black ink seared through the pages, striking through a good majority of my aunt's scrawled handwriting until it was a messy sea of words we would never get to read. *Why even bother*, my mother retorted, *sending this to us when we can't understand what it says anymore?*

I can't be a writer anymore. Not in this place where words are valued for so little, only appreciated when they serve as wind under the wings of leaders grappling to stay in control, waves that pummel my people with lies repeated so many times they begin to sound true.

The Party takes so much from us, but depriving our rights is the same reason so many of us have flocked to join them. Because if you do, you get everything back. If you simply feign approval on your face and heap praises upon political dialogue with your neighbors, you get it all. A telephone, a car (becoming one of the few who don't walk everywhere, although there's never anywhere to be), the freedom to write to your relatives and even *visit* them (unheard of, I know) – it's all yours.

My mother's younger brother joined. A few weeks ago, I heard. An ugliness took over her face when she spat the news out at the dinner table. I don't think we'll be seeing them anytime soon.

////////

27 April 1970

When I was younger, I would check each week for news from my uncle in America. Before the Party began to crack down on what type of correspondence we could receive and before his letters started to disappear from their regular place in our mailbox, I would bombard my parents with the constant question of *Has uncle sent us anything this week?* I would pour over his descriptions of the velvet curtains that shimmered under the brilliance of a hundred New York City stage lights, scanning the lines for recounts of his Saturday night

Vaudeville performances and dancing routines. My uncle, the professional ballet dancer, worked alongside Russian ballerinas and American actors. Juggling acts, animal shows, singers, and comedians all shared the same stage as he did.

His letters are what made me first fall in love with that country. *It's like a bubble gum machine*, he told us, as if anyone in the family could invent the faintest notion of what that American-sounding contraption was. *You know, the ones where you put the coin in, and you get back your gum. Fair trade, simple and straight up. Here, you put in the work, and you receive your reward. Money, fame, entertainment, all of it. It's not easy, but it sure is honest.* America was a place I could fill my days penning prose and singing the sweet sounds that clogged my thoughts on lazy Sunday mornings. It would give me all the space I needed to exist, to be.

I learned today that my uncle was more than just a dancer. I say *just a dancer* as if his profession does not fascinate me today as much as it did when I was a young boy. But he was so much more than I ever knew. When he escaped Albania, he came to New York City as a teen, with nothing more than a few dollars to his name, a handful of crisp bills sewn into a makeshift pocket he had made in the lining of his jacket so that they would not be taken along his journey. He sailed through Piraeus, the port city in Greece, and arrived in Ellis Island.

But when he got there, he stayed for one month before turning right back around. Because on the way there, he decided that it wasn't fair for him to be the only one to escape. Why should *he* be the lucky one? Why should he chase his dreams while everyone he had ever known and loved and everyone he hadn't yet gotten to know and love stayed behind?

And so he brought 1,650 of them back. Not all at once, of course, but over the span of two decades, he organized the escape of each and every single one of them, setting them up with apartments and jobs in restaurants across the city.

He came to my parents first, and asked them to move to America with him. And so they did. Today, I learned that I was born in the same country I placed on a pedestal all those years ago, the land I revered and admired thanks to my uncle's letters. But we're not in America now (obviously). My mother said it was something about politics and my father's work that brought them back so soon after they had left. I don't care to hear the details.

Today, April 27th, would have been my uncle's birthday. *Is* my uncle's birthday? He could still be alive, but to us, he's gone. We will never again hold his letters in our hands and hear him ramble on about the wonderful toppings with which he adorned his ice cream on a warm July afternoon. We can never rip open his envelope, crowding around as a family to hear about his chance encounter with an old Albanian friend or his long day at the meat market.

Today is also *my* birthday. We had that in common. I am sixteen now, which is how old my uncle was when he came to America. I suppose that's why my mother chose to tell me today, of all days. I cannot imagine that, leaving behind everything to escape a country that has told you *no, you aren't allowed to leave, you must stay here with the rest of us*. As restless as my life has left me, as devoid of dreams do I find myself, I don't think I could ever leave.

If I do, I hope I bring everyone with me. Like my uncle.

////////

30 April 1970

I am running out of pages now. It is alarming how quickly I fill these papers with words that mean nothing at all but everything to me. Funny how you don't ever notice something is coming to an end until you reach the ending for yourself, never having believed you would get there. Do we always take things for granted when they are granted freely at first, when we are tricked into thinking they would always be there?

I'm going to stop writing so frequently now. I will try not to open this book until I have something that needs to be written down, or until the longing in me to pick up my pen again becomes so overwhelming that I am willing to sacrifice the remaining empty space to quell that feeling.

////////

4 September 1972

The Party arrested my neighbors today.

I watched from my perch on the windowsill seat as they dragged them out of their house. The same house where I laughed over card games until I cried. The same house where I learned to properly knead the dough for *lakror*, because even though cooking was a girl's job, I wanted to learn. And my neighbors, with no kids of their own, were glad to teach me, understanding in all their kindness that this wasn't something I could ask my mother. The same house where I allowed my neighbors something in return: a person to whom they could justify themselves, justify their decision to join the Party all those years ago.

They had been some of the first to join, back when the Party was new, full of hope and the allure of fresh promises. The rewards for signing up were high then. My neighbors truly believed in all of it: a new life for themselves and everyone they could reach with the Party's message, rewarding those with bold convictions and even bolder dreams.

But none of it was enough. Not enough for my neighbors, and certainly not enough for the Party.

They said my neighbors said something critical of the government, and somebody reported them. It doesn't matter who. It never did. The Party fed on this sort of thing – the whispers that poked holes into even the most airtight loyalties, shaking the foundations of even the most steadfast relationships as friends turned on one another.

They arrested the couple today, sent them out to work in the fields as punishment.

It wasn't uncommon to be forced to pay out your apologies in the form of forced labor, far out in the countryside where nobody could hear you scream, even if you cried out loud enough. But it was the first time someone I truly knew went. My neighbors were like parents to me.

Twisting her head to catch one last glimpse of her house, the wife adopted a strange look of vacancy and regret. She had been crushed, but had nothing left in her to fight for it back.

Neither of my neighbors resisted. Nobody ever did. What was the point? When the Party came for you, you went. You didn't fight.

You just disappeared, to a world where your hands would blister and your back would break and people back home would shake their heads and cluck their tongues, afraid to feel anything but distance.

As the wheels of the truck kicked up dust on its drive away, I wanted to throw open the window and shout out to them. But of course I didn't, or I could have gone too.

I didn't cry either. I didn't even care that they were gone, and that scared me. But I couldn't, could I? Caring is a dangerous thing, and I've made the mistake of holding onto it for far too long. But I'm an adult now, the only man left in my family, and I can't cling to those childish practices any longer.

Emptiness echoes inside of me, but not as loudly as the restlessness. I need to get out, get away, run, leave. The fields have claimed my neighbors, just as they have claimed so many before them, and just as they will claim so many after. But they can't claim me. Not yet.

////////

5 September 1972

I remember now, that my grandfather almost had to go into the fields once. This was during the time of the Ottomans, not the Party. My father would always tell this story whenever he was trying to remind us kids to be grateful for what we had, even if it wasn't much at all. *They had beat him,* he would say, *tied him up and beat him in the village square. They were going to send him out to work in the fields too,* – at this, a shiver would run down our spines as we huddled together, waiting for the conflict to resolve – *until his little brother came running into the town's center. He waved a slip of paper over his head, hollering at the top of his lungs so that the Turks would look at him instead of your grandfather.*

These Ottomans had caught your grandfather speaking Albanian. Which would have been fine, except he had told them that he was a Greek. That's how you would get your kids into the Christian schools in those days, by proving that you were a Greek. Because they were fine to mess with us Albanians, but not the Greeks. Religion's never easy, huh? A sad twinkle in his eyes, but we never noticed back then. *If you weren't Greek, you had to be Muslim.*

So they tied him up, and his brother had to dash home, running so fast his calves burned and sent fire up his legs. He ran all the way there and all the way back, shoving those forged Greek papers into the Ottomans' hands so they would let his older brother go. And they did, but not without planting a fear so deep in his heart that it would remain there for all his years. The sad thing, though, is that they unknowingly planted a hatred as well. My father hated the Ottoman who tied him to that post. I mean, how could you not? But it wasn't just that one man that he hated. It was all of them.

He would never forget that day, and he would never let me forget. Now, I won't let you forget it, either. But I hope you take with you this lesson: never give someone a reason to hate you. Because, chances are, they will grow to hate everyone who reminds them of you, and it is a very selfish thing, to cause someone to hate that many people.

////////

17 February 1980

They left her.

My sister died in childbirth last year. The baby survived, but today, my sister's husband decided that a baby was not enough to tether him to our town for much longer, and he left her. Disappeared in the middle of the night, leaving nothing but a lengthy note on my doorstep explaining all the reasons he could not bear to stay, not even to watch over his own daughter. He asked me to take her in, to raise her as my own. It surprised me that he could not find it in himself to be a father, that becoming a parent had not clicked for him the way it did for so many others. I think his letter made me hate him, just a little. Not simply because he had abandoned her, but because he thought he could justify it with neat little letters arranged in rows on a page, empty excuses that grew wings and flew circles over my head as I tried to make sense of the words that said so much yet meant so little.

I am twenty-six now. Double my age when I first opened the pages of this book, when I first brought my pen to these papers and told myself who I was. As I was cleaning up today, I found this journal nestled between storage boxes upstairs, and I decided that I owed it to myself to fill these last pages in some way or another. This small luxury had once represented every luxury I sought from my future – a place to write as a profession, my only responsibility being to grasp onto as much fleeting adventure as I could store in the palms of my hands. The opportunity to see the world so that I could write about its wonders and tell the people I had seen them firsthand.

Here I am, now twenty-six, caring for little Emma. I am colder now than I once was. I do not know whether there is enough warmth for the both of us, but I will try. I will stay here for her because I have to. It is only right.

////////

9 August 1990

I have made a terrible mistake.

It scares me, that my mind is capable of such things, that my hands are capable of packing away my possessions to leave, that my eyes are capable of scanning the port waters for the ship, that my feet are capable of boarding a vessel that will bring me away from it all.

But what scares me more is that I do not regret it. I do not regret this mistake that I have made, and while the shame and the anxious yearning within me battle for ownership over my heart, I do not wince to see that regret is not one of them, that she offers up no fight in the matter.

I am thirty-six, and still I do not know what I am doing in my life. I hardly even know where I'm going, or if I will even get there.

All of these years I raised Emma, I was all that she had, and she filled that same role for me, the role of a thousand people who had come and gone, placed on this earth just to be taken away so soon. I loved her as much as I could allow. She was too young to notice, but there was a distance there, the weight of my restlessness wedging itself into the gaps between the hugs I gave her at night and the hands I wrapped around hers on the days loneliness enveloped her, a cruel blanket.

I had fear, too. Fear that I would leave her like her parents had. Fear that the wind would come and uproot me, for my roots weren't deeply planted in this earth. No, they never were. I suppose I was right to fear it, because it happened. Or maybe, my dreadful anticipation willed it into existence, filling my mind with thoughts of it so that I could do nothing but fulfill my fears. It is my fault, regardless. My mistake and mine alone.

It is 1990. We are ten years from a new century. Time is ticking. For the first time, the Party has granted us the right to travel abroad. The Party has crumbled. Crumbled under the weight of a thousand student protest signs, a thousand newspapers daring to tell the stories of new *political parties*, a thousand queue lines stretching around street corners, filled with a thousand grumbling voices unafraid to quiet their words for anyone any longer. It will be any day now, that it is over, never again to return. I did not want to stay behind to see the hope flicker again in people's eyes as they imagine a new life, a better life. I could not bear to be part of a people that will invent aspirations for themselves, never to see the light of day, always to remain as easy dreams.

Western embassies are helping some of the people flee. But I don't trust the politics of it all, and so I made different plans. I left with a friend from the next village over. We escaped to Durrës, whose sandy shores have seen the departures and arrivals of a million men and women, whose stretches of coastline have hosted the battles of Romans and Greeks who whispered a different name for the city under their breath: *Dyrrhachium*.

We seized a rusted ship and sailed illegally to Italy. I left her. I left Emma behind, and I hope she hates me for it, because hating is far better than hurting. I hope she never understands why I did it, because if she understands, then she must feel that same rustling impatience inside of her, and I hope she never feels the pressure of clipped wings the way that I do.

I have been in Italy for a month now. My own voyage, my own journey. I can write here, sing here, live here. Maybe I'll go to America, search for my uncle in the crowded throngs of New York City seas. It should excite me, and it does, I suppose. But it feels different when you don't know to whom you should extend your allegiance, when you are chasing dreams that are not full-fledged or even half-fledged. When you don't know whether you want better or simply what you can't have. I see now that there is a danger to curiosity when the feeling is aimless, without purpose or something to attach itself to, something to ground it.

It has been a month, and still I do not know what I want. It has been a month, and still I cannot rest at night, cannot sleep knowing that Emma is alone, cannot ease my mind when it understands that I placed my imaginings before hers. Each night, I think back to that day one month ago, when I left.

I never slept after that.

Made in United States
North Haven, CT
10 November 2024

60032151R00109